Secrets in the Silence

S Lynn C

Book Cover by Vikki

Formatting by: B Wills

ISBN: 979-8-9928401-7-9

TRIGGER WARNINGS

Due to Triggers of S/A and Aftermath. This work may contain content that may be triggering for some readers. Please read with caution

PLAYLIST

Ch 1 – Control – Too Close to Touch

Ch 2 – Sorry – Alan Walker

For the fans...

CONTENTS

Also by   477

PART ONE

Isabel

CHAPTER 1

I sat alone in the gloomy shadows, time dis-
solving around me. Curled into a ball, I let
the emptiness hold me in its cold, comforting embrace. My legs pulled tight to my chest, my head
buried deep into my arms.

I shook.

Not from cold. Not from fear.

From nothing.

A sudden touch on my back startled me. I lifted my head, eyes meeting hers, and my heart swelled with joy.

"Mom?" I tore away from her smile and jumped to my feet. Wrapping my arms around her as though she might float away. Her uniform brushed my cheek, familiar as she held me tightly. As we pulled away we were in our backyard, in Tennessee. She cupped my face in her hands, saying nothing, tears streaming down her face as she stared into my eyes. She smiled, but the sadness she held in her bright irises was unmistakable. I placed my hands over hers, a smile trembling onto my lips as tears welled. The warmth of her touch warmed my cheeks, like she was truly here.

"I miss you so much," I whispered, my voice trembling. She hugged me again, smoothing my hair with her hand before pressing a firm kiss to the top of my head.

When she released me, her warmth vanished. I was once again alone in the darkness. I could still feel the imprint of her kiss, and my heart sank deeper into despair as it faded.

"Mom?" I called, but there was no answer. She didn't return. I wiped the tears from my cheeks and looked around.

The darkness stretched on forever.

No escape in sight.

A ripple of air brushed past me, sending a chill down my spine. Despite that it felt familiar.

Comforting.

"Isabel." His voice was clear as day. I spun around.

"Jake?" The darkness was too thick to see through. "Jake, where are you?" The question echoed out into the vastness.

"Open your fucking eyes!" His voice cracked with desperation, laced with a fear I couldn't ignore.

"I can't." My voice cracked like glass, splintering into the void.

"Yes, you can." I wrapped my arms around myself and dropped my head, once again staring at my bare feet. I felt hands on my shoulders and looked up into his blue eyes. They were wide and full of desperation, like they had been that day on the cliff. I felt my heart lift almost immediately and his eyes softened, smiling slightly he pulled me into a hug. I untangled my arms from between us and wrapped them around him.

"Why did you come for me?" Tears pricked my eyes as the question left my lips.

I knew why.

But I was still angry with him for it.

He should be here.

We were supposed to face this head on, together. Solomon's trial was looming, and we were supposed to fight, now I was facing it alone.

"I'm always here for you." He rested his chin on my head.

He felt so real.

"But you're not here," I said softly, my heart shattering with the truth. I felt his hand on the back of my head before he ran it down my hair.

"I'm never far."

"But I need you, here." I stopped. My mind was searching for what I needed to tell him. "Something happened." I pulled away, confusion furrowed on my brow. I looked into the emptiness. "But I can't remember what it was." Screaming erupted in the back of my mind.

Shrill.

Fearful.

Desperate.

I closed my eyes willing it to stop, as I covered my ears. I felt Jake's tension as he hugged me again. The screaming silenced.

"You will." He pulled away from me, my eyes flicked open, meeting his and simultaneously a bright light appeared off in the distance.

"What is that?" I asked, turning to look at the light. Returning my gaze to him, he cupped my cheek. A single tear slid down his face as a small smile appeared.

"You need to go."

"I want to stay here with you and mom." I felt the tears coming again, heavier this time. He swiped his thumbs along my cheeks as he cupped my face firmly.

"Isabel, you have to wake up."

"I don't want to." My words were a desperate plea as my last lucid memories surfaced. Jake's eyes were sad.

He knew.

He pulled me tightly to him. The bright light rushed towards us. I wrapped my arms around him, not wanting to let him go. The brightness shrouded us, and I was instantly blinded.

It was the wind kissing my lashes, that made my eyes flutter open. Staring up at the cloudy sky as the sun hid itself, as though it wished not to bear witness to the heinous act that had befallen me. There were no birds in the sky, there was nothing but silence's companionship. There was a ringing in my ears that made my head spin. Moving my sore eyes around I could see that I was alone. I tried to draw in a full breath, but my body only allowed short, shallow sips of air. A harsh cough tore from my chest.

The world tilted.

The air had the smell of autumn but was tainted by the strong scent of iron

One I was familiar with.

Blood.

Slowly, I forced myself up as pain vented through my body. My throat burned with every breath. My face throbbed where shattered glass had kissed my skin. I painfully reached my arm up to grab the bumper of the truck and used it to pull myself from the ground. My legs wobbling beneath me. I looked up into the sky as tears pricked my eyes, fear gripping at me as I tried to avoid looking down.

Taking a deep breath, I looked down. Jake's oversized t-shirt was all that remained, covered in blood. There was blood on my bare feet, bloody cuts and bruises going up my legs from the involuntary spasms. I closed my eyes and could see my legs kicking away.

Scraping for escape.

I opened my eyes. I had to get away from here.

Away from *him*.

Shakily, using the tailgate to aid me I took a step and felt a sickly stickiness between my thighs. A sob tore from my throat, raw and burning, stealing what little air I had left. Leaning against the truck I put my hands above my head, like Jake used to after he ran. Tears ran down my face as the pain coursed through my body. The shake in my chest burned with every breath. My mind was racing, knocking against the walls of my skull, as everything that happened came to the forefront.

Screams again echoed from the quiet. I forced a deep breath.

The pain became more tolerable and my breathing steadied, despite the lightheadedness that had ensued. I turned my head, looking at the house as it sat in the dim light, beckoning me towards it, silently.

I had to get to the house.

Managing a few steps, I made my way along the side of the truck, sliding along it slowly, shards of the broken window cracking and stabbing the bottoms of my feet as I stepped through it. At the driver side where the window was now missing, a flash of being slammed into it appeared in my mind's eye as the sound of shattering glass echoed out into the obscure silence that surrounded me.

Reaching the front of Jake's truck, I pushed myself upright, preparing to take a step toward the house.

Letting go; I wrapped my arms tightly around myself as I slowly took a step forward. The pain continuously pulsing in my body, like a vein.

I managed a few steps before my body betrayed me. My muscles locked, and I crashed down.

Wet, ragged breaths pulling from my chest.

"Isabel?" My name gently danced across the silence, followed by a sharp gasp. Slowly raising my eyes, they landed on Meg. She was standing on the porch, her backpack slung over her shoulder. I forgot she was supposed to come over for homework after she finished soccer practice. Her backpack slid from her still frame, hitting the deck with a loud thud. The sound broke her free from her trance and she dashed down the stairs towards me. She stopped just a few feet away from me.

It was written all over her face.

She approached me slowly, as though I were a wounded animal. My body trembled as our eyes met, and fresh tears began to rim my eyes. Slowly, she knelt in front of me, taking me gently by the arms. My hands shakily grabbed hers in response and I could feel my entire body ripple with a painful shudder.

"What happened?" she asked as she brushed a painful cut by my eye with the back of her hand. I shrank away at her touch, and she pulled her hand away, quietly placing it back on my arm. I opened my mouth to speak.

My lips moved.

The words were forming.

But nothing was coming out.

My eyes widened at the realization that I no longer had a voice. I didn't understand, I had just spoken with my mom and Jake when I was with them. I scanned Meg's face, maybe she could hear me, but I couldn't hear myself. Her eyes left mine drifting to my neck. Her gaze snapped back up to me, and I could see the unavoidable tears rippling down her cheek. She gripped my arms firmly and took a shaky breath.

"We need to get you out of here," she said as she slowly nodded her head. Her face was blurred by the hot tears that were relentlessly assaulting my eyes. I nodded but found myself unable to move.

I was frozen to the spot. My eyes fell to the ground when she tilted my chin up and my eyes found hers again. "We need to get you some help. Do you want me to call your Dad?"

Dad. He was going to be so upset with me. I looked over her shoulder to the house, to make sure he wasn't somehow already here. I had no idea what time it was, but the last thing I wanted was for my Dad to see me like this. It was bad enough that Meg was the one to find me. I shook my head and hung it.

"Can you stand up?" she asked, as she stood. I looked up at her and slowly nodded my head. She held steadily to my arms to get me up, when I quickly realized that I was too weak to help her. Another wave of pain washed through me, and I exhaled sharply. Meg knelt down again and pulled me against her. Hugging me tightly, my head resting on her shoulder, the tears continued to fall. I felt her shift slightly. Everything around me began to spin again and I became more reliant on her bracing me. She had one arm around my shoulders, and the other had managed to fish her phone from her back pocket. I could hear the dial tone sounding from her speaker.

"Appomattox county nine-one-one, what is the nature of your emergency?"

"Yes, I need help at fifty-two-eighty-six forest hill road."

"What's going on?" Meg hugged me tighter.

"My friend has been assaulted."

It wasn't much longer after she had hung up the phone, that I heard sirens in the distance. I was still resting my head on Meg's shoulder, her arms still tightly around me, unwilling to let go. We sat in the silence, only accompanied by the symphony of rustling leaves from those that remained on the trees, as the autumn breeze danced through them. A whirlwind caught my attention briefly in the distance, distracting my troubled mind.

The tumultuous thoughts returned when I saw the police cruisers, lights flashing and the distant resonating wail of their sirens, followed by the ambulance, shooting up the road towards the house. With a staggered breath, the world began to slip out of focus again.

CHAPTER 2

The hiss of the ambulance doors decompressing was what woke me. I was rushed into a room as the shades snapped shut over the windows. As they closed the door, I could see Meg, standing in the hallway, with her arms wrapped around herself, tears staining her face. They quickly transferred me from the gurney on to the bed, leaving the sheet, the paramedics had clearly draped over my visibly damaged body.

"Get a warm blanket," one of the nurses instructed. I watched another nurse nod, and she disappeared quickly, before returning and draping something warm and heavy overtop of me. Lying in bed, despite the warm blanket's weight, my body shook. Looking up at the lights above, I could feel his hand touching my bare skin, his laugh as my legs stilled in the dirt beneath him before. The door slid open, breaking me free of the vicious memory and I turned my head to see an officer walking in. The nurses stood firm around the bed, almost as if they were protecting me.

"We would like to get a statement if she is up for it," he said. One of the nurses took my hand and my eyes flicked to her.

"Can you give a statement?" I looked at the officer, before reaching for my throat and looking back at the nurse. I wanted them to know who had done this to me, but my voice was gone. Her eyes shifted slightly to my neck before she looked back up to the officer.

"I don't think she will be able to give you a statement at this time."

"We will be outside waiting." She nodded and he left the room. She turned back to me.

"Is there anyone you want us to call?" I knew it was time to call my Dad, although I didn't want to. I opened my mouth to speak but again nothing came out as I formed the words. She quickly produced a pen and a little notebook from her breast pocket. I quickly wrote down Dad's phone number. Handing it back, she took it from me gently, before softly taking my hand and looking me in my eyes.

"We're going to take care of you, okay?" I nodded my head, and she squeezed my hand sympathetically.

Time seemed to tick by; I was thankful that I was never alone as one nurse always stayed in the room with me. The door began to slide open, and my heart pounded in my chest as my Dad stepped into the room. His eyes met mine and upon meeting, the alarm he held in them vanished, replaced with a mixture of relief and sadness. His chest was heaving as though he had run all the way here. I glanced away quickly, shame filling me as his eyes remained on me. I heard shuffling as he got closer to the bed. He slowly sat down on the edge and reached for my hand, but I pulled it away.

He pulled his hand back as though he were afraid.

I couldn't bring myself to look at him.

I was disgusting.

Ruined.

I didn't deserve his comfort.

"Isabel." His voice cracked as he said my name. I still refused to look up. "I should have been there." His voice shook. I wasn't sure how much he knew, but the sound of his voice was either disappointment or guilt. Keeping my eyes cast down I shook my head no. I squeezed them shut as fresh tears began to fall and then I felt a gentle hand on my chin, guiding my head upwards. I opened my eyes and tears stained his cheeks, weaving through the stubble that had since grown from this morning.

The door opened again, both of us looking at the doctor walking in. Beyond that in the hallway, I could see two police officers standing. No doubt, waiting for the opportunity to get a statement. My throat began to burn with the desire to speak the words out loud, for them to take them down and do what they could. The doctor stepped in quietly and slowly walked towards me. Dad stood from the bed and stepped aside so she could get closer.

"I'm Dr. Morgan. Follow the light please." She flashed a light in my eyes, moving it around and I followed it, despite the throbbing in my face with each movement.

"Schedule a CT scan for head trauma, her eyes are lethargic, could be nothing, but I want to be sure." I looked at Dad as he stood off to the side listening intently.

"Yes, doctor." She turned the light off and tipped my head backwards gently, my neck and head aching as she did so.

"Open as wide as you can for me," she instructed. I opened my mouth, but only slightly as the pain ripped from the motion. She took her flashlight and looked inside. She sighed as she turned her flashlight off.

"Also schedule an MRI. Page Dr. Francis, I want her to check the larynx, these bruises are severe."

"Right away doctor." She let go of my chin and I straightened my head, looking at her. Her eyes held strength, despite already knowing deep down what had happened to me. She stepped back.

"You must be her father."

"Yes, ma'am."

"You can sit back down now," she said, Dad closed the gap and sat down on the edge of the bed, taking my hand in his. He looked down and I saw him, eyeing the scrapes on my knuckles, he ran his thumb over them cautiously as it began to tremble.

"I have a few questions for you, so I can determine the course of treatment." I nodded my head; it throbbed heavily as I sat there. The distant sound of glass shattering as the image of hitting the driver side window of Jake's truck echoed in my mind. I suddenly felt the crushing pressure radiate through my throat, and I reached for his hand to stop it, but the only hand there was my own.

"Can you speak?" I opened my mouth and formed words but only air came and a shallow breathy huff from frustration.

I shook my head no.

Dad squeezed my hand for comfort.

She cleared her throat and shifted uncomfortably.

"This question won't be easy, but I have to ask."

I nodded, knowing full well what was to come next.

"Were you sexually assaulted?" Her words were firm, but there was a hint of a shake behind them.

She felt as uncomfortable asking as I did answering.

The words rang through my ears and echoed in my head.

The pain in my body raged and I shifted uncomfortably.

Dad's eyes met mine and I could see within them he was pleading for me to shake my head no. The tears welled heavily again, and I dropped my gaze to my lap, letting them run down my cheeks as I shook my head yes.

"Oh my God," he sighed heavily. I felt his hand leave mine and move to the back of my head, gently pulling me to his chest and holding me tightly against him.

"Mr."

"Twain. Michael Twain."

"Mr. Twain, as Isabel is a minor, it is up to you if you would like for us to perform a SAFE exam."

Dad kissed the side of my head and turned his attention to Dr. Morgan.

"What is that?"

"Sexual Assault Forensics Exam, it helps preserve any evidence." Dad looked down at me and my eyes met his.

"Was it him?" he asked. I knew right away he was referring to Solomon, despite him being behind bars, there was no telling what that man was capable of.

I shook my head no.

The pain in his eyes was evident.

"What if she doesn't want to do it?" Dad asked, returning his attention to Dr. Morgan.

"It's your decision. In this case, I would recommend it, from just what I am seeing, your daughter is incredibly lucky to be alive." Dad squeezed his eyes shut again and turned his head back to me.

He looked at me, and I could see the battle he held, holding back the tears.

"Do you want to do this?" He had to make the decision, but I knew he wouldn't make me do it, if I didn't want to. I wanted Solomon's brother to be caught, so this wouldn't happen to anyone else. I shook my head yes. He turned back to Dr. Morgan. "Schedule the exam please." She nodded quietly. Her eyes met mine again.

"Isabel, are your cycles regular?" I nodded.

"I'll put an order in for a dose of Levonorgestrel." I felt Dad's head move in her direction.

"What's that?" Dad asked. She shifted uncomfortably.

"It's the morning after pill. In a situation like this, it's safer to administer it, to eliminate the risk of an unwanted pregnancy. I'll also need your consent for that as well." He shook at her words, rage emanating from deep within his chest.

"I consent." His reply was strained. "She's been through enough; that's the last thing she needs." I felt myself shaking against Dad's chest and his arms grew tighter, almost like being squeezed by a boa constrictor. Tears seeping into his shirt as I cried silently. I just wanted it all to stop. Dad ran his hand down the back of my head, smoothing my hair, shushing me quietly.

"They'll take her for imaging now," the doctor said quietly. "Dr. Francis will be here soon."

"Thank you." Dad whispered. She nodded her head again before quietly leaving the room.

His arms tightened around me, and I crumbled.

I wanted to tell him how sorry I was for letting this happen to me.

That I had disappointed him and broken his heart, again.

The desire to speak to him was massively overwhelming and all I could manage was to sob.

He pulled away and gently cupped my cheeks with his hands, trying to brush away the tears as fast as they fell to no avail. He pulled me back against him again, planting a hard kiss on top of my head. He sniffled as he held me.

"It's going to be okay. Daddy's here." The sobs came harder, making my head, eyes, and throat burn.

Shame coiled tight in my chest.Every ugly thought clawed at me at once.

What I should have done.

What I hadn't done.

Every rule I had broken.

I folded inward beneath it, unable to escape my own mind.

My mind trailed to Jake.

I was afraid he would be disappointed in me.

He would never look at me the same way again had he been alive and here.

Another explosion of wracked sobs came from my chest at the thought of my brother. I needed him, but at the same time, I was grateful he wasn't here to see this.

To see what had been done to me.

To see the shame clinging where it didn't belong.

My body folded against his as the sobs took over. He quietly shushed me as he began to gently rock me side to side once more.

The room around us pulsed with the urgency of the hospital beyond the door, filling every lingering moment with anxiety.

It wasn't much longer that a nurse entered. She nodded to the one that had been standing silently in the corner like a statue on guard, before looking at me with soft eyes.

"It's time to go," she said quietly. Dad let go of me although I could feel that he didn't want to. He leaned down and kissed my forehead gently before he stepped away from the bed so they could take me. They unlocked the wheels, the locks slamming hard out of position, sending shivers up my spine.

"When will she be back?"

"After the imaging tests, they want us to take her for the SAFE, that alone is several hours. Dr. Francis, will also examine her, it could be awhile."

"Can I wait here?"

"Of course, sir." Dad nodded and looked at me again, taking my hand and squeezing it gently.

"I'll see you when you get back." I nodded and then he let go, stepping back so they could maneuver the bed out of the room.

As we got into the hallway, I could see Meg sitting in a chair, her head in her hands. I reached my hand out towards her.

"Do you want to stop?" The nurse asked. I nodded my head and pointed at Meg. She walked over to Meg and gently touched her on the shoulder. I watched them engage, just before Meg turned her eyes to mine. Getting up she came over and took my hand.

"You're going to be okay," she sniffled, her eyes were red and rimmed with tears. Hot tears ran down my face as I looked up at her, the light making her hair appear on fire. I nodded and squeezed her hand gently.

"I'll see you when you come back." Hands appeared on her shoulders, and she turned her head as my eyes landed on my Dad.

"You can keep me company while we wait. You should probably call your folks as well, I'm sure they are worried about you." She nodded and then turned her eyes back to me and squeezed my hand, before letting go. I held her gaze briefly as the tears blurred her, before looking up to my Dad. I didn't want to leave them, part of me didn't want to go through with the exam, but I knew that if I didn't do it, and he remained out there, he could do it to someone else. I took a shuddered breath as Dad wiped away my tears.

"I love you," he whispered. I opened my mouth and formed I love you in return. A small smile creased in the corner of his lips, and he took my hand, kissing it.

"Ready?" the nurse asked. I sighed heavily, nodding. Dad squeezed my hand.

He hesitated before letting go. His eyes betraying him as his tear rimmed eyes were now a brilliant red in the light. Once more the bed was moving down the hallway, before turning a corner where Dad and Meg disappeared.

The hallways were quiet and cold. The warm blanket they had given me before we left the room seemed to have lost all of its heat almost immediately.

I had no idea what was about to happen.

But it had to be done.

CHAPTER 3

The same nurses who had been with me since my arrival remained with me as they did the exam. They explained everything that they needed to do to complete the test. It was going to take some time, but they needed to be diligent to get the best evidence possible. There would be some prodding, swabbing and pictures taken. At the thought of them taking pictures of me I trembled. Seeing this the nurse took my hand and squeezed it gently.

"I know it's a lot, but this is the best way to make sure that whoever did this to you can never hurt anyone else again." I felt my throat burn as she spoke. I would believe it when I see it.

"This is for my brother." His sickening voice echoed in my mind. He was Solomon's brother and if Solomon was able to elude the law for as long as he had, then I had no doubt in my mind that his vicious brother could afford the same. Her gentle squeeze on my hand broke me from my thoughts and I could see her clearly.

"Are you ready?" I managed to shudder a sigh and shook my head.

The pictures and the needles were the easy part. They even scraped under my nails and collected any debris they found, hoping it might contain some identifiable DNA. The hardest part came when they asked me to lie down. My heart pounded in my chest as I did so, and they gently placed my legs in stirrups. Violent tremors tore through me as panic stole my breath. A sweet-eyed nurse approached me and took my hand. My eyes met hers as silent tears fell slowly down my cheek.

"This is going to be uncomfortable, but we are almost done. I'm going to be right here." I nodded, and shortly after there was a painful pressure. I closed my eyes as my breathing quickened, and she squeezed my hand again. I could feel tears turning to ice against my cheek as they rolled down in the cold room. The room folded in on itself, dragging me back to the backyard with him. The urge to run consumed me until a gentle hum broke through the chaos. I turned to look at her again. She quietly began to sing. As my thoughts scattered in every direction, I couldn't make out what she was singing, but it was soothing, slowly calming my mind, and allowing me to take calming breaths.

As they finished up, I put a hospital gown on and returned to the bed. The nurse covering me with a fresh warming blanket, a welcome comfort after being completely exposed in the cold room.

The room was quiet aside from the soft foot-steps of the nurses around me as they labeled and packed up the bags of evidence. A knock echoed through the room, startling me. It opened slowly and another doctor entered the room.

"Dr. Morgan requested me for a throat consult."

"Yes, Dr. Francis, this is Isabel." She approached me, examining the bruises to my throat carefully as she got closer.

"Isabel, can you tell me what happened?" I shook my head no.

"She can't speak." Dr. Francis looked at the table, the evidence bags being packed away.

"Open your mouth for me." I opened it as wide as I could, despite the pain that followed and she looked down in, putting a stick on my tongue to see.

Taking the stick out she turned off her light and sighed. She gently pressed her fingers in various places on my neck, checking the bruising.

"I'll need to perform a laryngoscopy to be sure, but I'd almost bet based on the bruising and your inability to talk that you have severely damaged vocal chords." My eyes burned as she spoke, meeting hers with so many questions that I couldn't even ask.

"Try not to worry for now." She patted my hand that rested gently in my lap. "Once I get in there and take a look we won't know much, but you need to prepare yourself. This is a very delicate injury that will require some therapy as you recover." I nodded my head, and she turned to leave.

Stopping she acknowledged the nurse near the door.

"Get her on my schedule for first thing tomorrow morning."

"Yes, Doctor." She exited the room, and a new wave of fresh tears began to stream down my face.

"Don't cry. She's one of the best in the area and she will do whatever it takes to help give you your voice back." I nodded and she hugged me gently.

My body was sore, but the hug was more than welcomed.

They took me back in a wheelchair, and I quickly realized we went an unusual way. Instead of taking me back to the room where they had retrieved me from, they took me into a private room. Dad was sitting in a chair, and Meg was soundly sleeping on the couch. He stood as they began to wheel me through the door.

As they stopped, Dad walked around, gently taking my hands in his and helping me up from the chair. My body ached as he helped me stand before he slowly helped me get into the bed.

"Dr. Francis has her scheduled for a laryngoscopy, in the morning."

"What time?"

"Someone will be in to get her around seven-thirty." Dad nodded and looked down at me.

"Are you okay?" he asked. I nodded, despite the torment running rampant through my mind. I looked at the clock; it was already after midnight. He turned back to the nurses.

"Thank you." The one who had pushed the wheelchair nodded before she walked back out into the hallway, the one who stuck with me all day stood.

"You're welcome, if you need anything, I will be here."

"What's your name?"

"Sarah."

"Thank you, Sarah, for taking care of her." Sarah nodded quietly and then left the room. Dad gently sat down next to me on the bed, and I glanced over at Meg.

"I tried to convince her to have her folks come get her, but she refused to leave." I looked back at him and painfully cocked an eyebrow. I could feel the butterfly bandages they had placed over the cut stretch as I did.

"They know she's here." He sighed and put a hand on my shoulder. I tensed under his touch although it was warm, it wasn't deliberate. I was a disgrace and yet he was trying to comfort me. His eyes didn't leave mine and the pain of my reaction was immediate. He pulled his hand away and stood up from the side of the bed.

My heart broke.

I didn't mean to hurt him, and I knew it wasn't him.

It was all me.

Every broken thought told me I should have fought harder.

I reached out and grabbed his hand. He knelt down beside me and pulled it to his lips, kissing it gently. He looked into my eyes, like he was trying to read my mind. Pushing stray strands of hair out of my face, he sighed.

"This isn't your fault." My eyes welled with tears. As one slipped down my cheek he swiped it away with his thumb. I felt my chest rattle, and I threw my arms around him. He stood slightly and encircled me in his arms. "You did what you could. The important part is that you're safe now and you are going to be okay. With time you will overcome this." I nodded against him, and he kissed the top of my head. He pulled away and wiped away more tears, before resting his hands on my shoulders, squeezing them gently.

"Get some sleep, we'll see you in the morning," he said. I nodded and he went to take a seat in the chair. I looked at the door, panic ensuing. "Don't worry, I'll be right here. No one will hurt you, not while I'm around." I looked at him again and I could see that he was prepared to stay up all night if he had to. I nodded and rested my head back against the pillows. Their softness cradling my throbbing head, pulling me into sleep.

There was heavy breathing. I opened my eyes ever so slightly, light filtering in, enveloping the silhouette of the man. As his face became clear, he looked down at me and smiled. Pain was raising hell in my body. I heard a slight gasp come from my parted lips as I tried to breathe.

I needed to get away.

Terror ripped through me and my body reacted before my mind could.

I began thrashing.

My eyes rolled back, bringing the darkness forward.

I shot up. My mouth open in a scream as nothing came out, tears rushing down my face as I could still feel him on top of me. I was ripping at the blankets trying to get them off.

Trying to get *him* off.

Dad was on his feet and encircled his arms around me instantly, despite my thrashing. He pulled my head to his chest, resting his head on top of mine, I could feel the stubble on his chin.

Panic detonated inside my chest with nowhere to go.

"I got you," he said hoarsely. My mind flickered back to another time when I was held the same way, by Uncle Ben, the day my brother died. I could feel my mind unraveling; all of the memories that were playing back were like getting shot again, watching my brother die and *him*.

My chest locked with every silent scream.

I felt Dad shift and before I knew it the door swung open, and a nurse ran in followed by Sarah. Dad was quickly on his feet as he stepped away from me.

"What happened?" Sarah asked.

"I don't know. She's inconsolable." Sarah quickly went around the bed and connected something to my finger. I heard the monitor come to life.

"Her heart rate is dangerously high, I need point three milligrams of Midazolam," Sarah said. My eyes followed the other nurse as she reached into a cabinet nearby and pulled fluid into a syringe.

"Hold on sweetie, it's going to be okay," Sarah cooed with a slight panic in her voice. I looked to Dad as he had his arms wrapped around himself, tears silently falling as there was nothing he could do to help me. How horrific, knowing your child is in pain and terrified, only to not be able to protect them. How could he even begin to protect me, when the most dangerous villain in the room was my own thoughts? I couldn't even begin to imagine what he was thinking or feeling. I threw my hands forward in protest. Sarah gently took hold of my arms, holding them still as the needle pinched, breaking through my skin.

Everything began to blur.

My eyes fluttered and I fell back against the bed.

Dad's face was the last thing I saw before the world went out.

When I woke up, daylight had replaced the dark. Sunlight was cascading in from the window behind me, illuminating Dad and Dr. Francis, casting their shadows on the wall. Their voices stayed barely above a whisper. I opened my mouth to speak, then closed it again, remembering there was no point. I raised my arm and dropped it heavily on the bed with a thump. Dad and Dr. Francis looked at me. He approached the bed and took my hand in his.

"There she is," he said softly, pushing strands of hair out of my face. My body was achy; I looked at Dr. Francis, and she came closer to the bed.

"We took a look at your throat this morning." I swallowed with difficulty, hearing the gulp. "There is severe damage to your vocal cords, as I suspected." I took a deep breath, a whistle pitching from my parted lips as I waited for her to continue. Dad squeezed my hand for reassurance. I looked into his eyes and could see tears. "We are going to start you in speech therapy, with the hopes of getting your voice back. Right now, you need to rest and try not to talk or speak in any way. This will be a long road, but recovery is possible." I looked back at Dr. Francis, holding my hand up as though I was writing. She pulled a notepad and pen from her coat pocket and handed it to me. I slowly scratched across the paper, my hand sore, the scrapes, and bruises on my knuckles obtrusive in the glaring sun.

"How long?" I held the pad out and she glanced over it quickly.

"I can't say for sure," she sighed heavily.

"What are my chances of getting it back?" I wrote. She looked at the paper. Standing straight she took her glasses off and rubbed her eyes. Pulling her hand away from her face she looked at Dad before returning her eyes to meet mine. Dad squeezed my hand again, preparing me.

"Less than thirty percent."

The room tilted as her words hit.

I was being erased.

One syllable at a time.

I looked at Dad.

"Don't worry, we are going to do everything we can," he said softly.

"I've seen people with far greater damage get their voice back," Dr. Francis said. I scratched on the paper again.

"How long until they got it back?" Her eyes flicked to Dad and then back to me.

The look she held deep within her caramel irises, made my breath hitch.

"Years."

CHAPTER 4

As Dad unlocked and pushed open the front door the next morning, I hesitantly stepped up to the threshold. The house felt wrong the moment the door opened. Dad waited patiently beside me, but stepping inside felt impossible.

Last time, I had Jake.

This time, I was on my own.

Yes, terrible things had happened to us.

The physical pain would heal in time, but the mental and emotional toll on me would remain forever. I never could have imagined that the next time I stepped through this door, I'd be a completely different person and not by choice.

I jumped slightly as Dad put his hands on my shoulders. He rubbed my arms.

"You can do this," he whispered. I nodded and stepped inside. Although the world was crashing down inside me, I forced a smile. He walked by me, and his keys made a metallic clink as they fell into the dish on the hallway stand. I jumped slightly at the sound, but he didn't seem to notice. He walked down the hall and into the kitchen.

I made sure the door was locked before following him.

In the kitchen, he started the coffee pot, while I sat down at the table, resting my chin on my arms, watching him. An uneasiness crawled through my blood as my back was exposed to the openness of the room. I got up and moved my chair so that my back was towards the wall. He heard me moving and glanced over his shoulder, a sigh escaping him.

Quiet.

Heavy.

He opened a drawer, pulling out a pad of paper and a pen. Walking over to the table he set them down in front of me.

"I need you to write out what you remember, the police still want to get a statement from you, and I don't think we should wait much longer."

I stared at them.

How could I tell him?

It was going to break him.

Reaching out, I pulled them towards me.

Picking up the pen, I scratched the paper.

Every word, making me ache.

"He's Solomon's brother." Tears began to stream heavily down my face as I read the words on the paper before turning it around for Dad to see. His words, "This is for my brother," echoed menacingly in my head. Dad's eyes widened as they remained on the paper for much longer than they should have. He looked up at me bewildered.

"Are you certain?" I nodded my head and pulled the paper back towards me to scratch out something else.

"He asked me if I really thought bars would keep Solomon from getting to me and that this was for his brother." I slid the notepad back to Dad and he stared at it. I wrapped my arms around myself, grabbing my elbows, making myself as small as possible. His head dropped lower, and he sighed heavily. I could see his fist clenching on the table. When he looked back up at me, he had tears in his eyes. He pushed himself off the table and over to me, where he got down on his knees next to me. I quickly turned in my chair as I was overcome with grief and he grabbed me into a tight hug, my arms pinned between us as he held my head tightly against his chest. I could hear his heartbeat.

Strong.

Unsteady.

Like instead of beats, it was the sound of breaking.

I sobbed silently on his shoulder.

"I'm so sorry, Isabel. I should have been here." His voice was hoarse, and a sniffle followed his words. I felt myself shaking in his embrace and pulled my arms out, wrapping them around him, hugging him tighter. I needed to feel secure and right now I felt vulnerable. Solomon's brother had a choice, and he chose the worst outcome.

Letting me live had been the cruelest choice he could've made.

I could feel my heart pounding in my chest, and I began gasping for air.

Dad pulled away standing up and immediately walked out of the kitchen and into the bathroom. He brought back an inhaler. The medicine burned down my throat, forcing air back into lungs that didn't want it yet. Dad fetched a water bottle from the fridge, opened it, and gave it to me.

"Sip, slowly," he instructed. I nodded and took small sips. The icy water, freezing the fire in my throat, trickling all the way down to my stomach. Putting the water back on the table, Dad returned the cap to it. He knelt down in front of me again and cupped my face, rubbing my cheek gingerly with his thumb.

"He won't get away with this. I promise you." I nodded and he pulled me into another hug. When he pulled away, he headed to the stove, and I saw him pull a box of mashed potatoes from the cabinet above. Dr. Francis's parting instructions lingered in my mind.

"Soft foods for a few weeks, after the pain settles and you are able to eat solids, we will get you into therapy, so we can get a head start," she had said. I had nodded and Dad shook her hand, thanking her before we headed out the door. Returning to the kitchen at the sound of the saucepan hitting the stove, I rested my head on my arms and watched as Dad navigated the kitchen.

When he put the plate in front of me, it held mashed potatoes and scrambled eggs. My stomach turned as I looked at it. I wasn't very hungry. I turned to him and forced a small smile. I was appreciative of his efforts, but I was unsure if I could force myself to eat, afraid that my body would revolt and make the situation far worse.

"I need you to try," he said softly, taking a seat across the table from me. I nodded and picked up the fork, pushing the eggs around as my stomach grumbled and wanted to reject itself at the same time. Picking up a small amount, I took the bite. The pain in my jaw came from what used to be the easy task of simply opening my mouth, evident as I slowly chewed.

After eating, I was lying on the couch when there came a knock at the door. I practically threw myself off as I sat up, pure fear coursing through my veins. Dad stood from his chair.

"Stay right there." He put his hand out, signaling for me to stay. I nodded and pulled my legs up against me as my chest heaved. Dad walked to the door; his heavy footsteps, thundering loudly in my mind with every step he took. I heard him unlocking it before he opened it.

"Chuck."

"Mike." I heard footsteps approaching. Dad soon reappeared with the Sheriff following behind him.

"Please have a seat," Dad said as he pointed out the chair, before joining me on the couch. He put his arm around my shoulders and hugged me tightly to his side. The Sheriff removed his hat as he sat down. He regarded me quietly and I could see that there was sadness in his eyes. He had been so helpful with everything regarding Solomon, he was always coming by with updates, and this was probably the last thing he expected to happen.

"The hospital sent over the results from the exam."

"They gave us the results before we left, they said they found DNA," Dad said.

"Yes, they did, and they sent it to us to run it through our database, and we got a hit."

"Who? Who did this to my daughter?" His voice was laced with urgency. I looked up at him.

He already knew.

What he wanted was a name.

Something solid to carry the rage that had nowhere else to go

I looked at the Sheriff as he sat there uncomfortably. He looked down at the hat in his hands as he fidgeted with it.

"The DNA came back to Soren Cross. Solomon's younger brother."

The taste of iron filled my mouth at the sound of *his* name, making my stomach turn.

I felt Dad's chest rise and fall heavily.

"How fast can you bring him in?"

"Mike, it's not that simple. Soren Cross has been on the radar nationwide." I folded into myself as he spoke. Every word stacked another weight on my chest. "Not just for assaults, but for other things. Just like Solomon."

"But what are you guys doing right now, actively to find him?"

"We don't have much to go on right now. We're reviewing the camera footage you gave us from your security system, and we've been interviewing people from the HVAC company."

"Did you ask his brother?"

"Solomon has received no correspondence from anyone, and no letters have gone out. He hasn't even made a phone call, his lawyer visits in person."

"What about people in his cell block? There has to be someone that got out recently that could have helped orchestrate this."

"We are tracking down everyone who was in the same block as him that has been released, but there aren't many as most of them with him are lifers."

"That is the only way I can think that this could have happened," Dad said, his grip on me tightening protectively.

"We are doing everything we can, Mike. Soren will mess up again and when he does, we are going to nail him." A shiver went up my spine with the thought that he was going to attack someone else. I pulled away from Dad and quickly got up from the couch. Rushing into the kitchen, I grabbed the pen and paper off the table and went back into the living room. I scratched on the piece of paper.

"What if he comes back?" I handed it to the sheriff, and he looked at it quickly.

"I can't tell you he won't. This case is different from the others he was tied to."

"Different how?" Dad asked.

"His other victims. He has a type. Dark hair, dark eyes, between twenty and thirty. All of them were beaten, and they were random. Isabel is the only minor that he has ever attacked according to his record. She's also the first one that he strangled.

This wasn't just a random attack. This was per-sonal." I felt heat flare up in my face at his words.

"So, he might not come back, if he doesn't know she survived, then he would have no reason to return," Dad said. I scribbled on the paper.

"He knows I'm alive." I showed it to Dad and his eyes met mine.

"Are you sure?" I turned the notepad, scribbling with a heavy hand as anxiety weighed me down.

"I woke up." He read it and he cleared his throat, forcing back the tears that were welling in his eyes. He pulled me closer to him, the paper rustling as it fell to the floor.

I could feel him shake.

Not out of sadness.

But pure rage.

"For now, I would recommend keeping a low profile." I felt Dad's chest rumble as he took a deep breath.

"I'm not going to let her out of my sight."

I glanced up at him, and his eyes held determination, along with a fragility that I had never seen before.

For the first time, I realized my fear wasn't mine alone.

CHAPTER 5

F rustration rose in me as I tried to speak the words that were on the chart in front of me with nothing coming out. Falling back against the chair, I huffed loudly. Joy sat forward, putting her hands on the table gently.

"It's okay. This is going to take some time." Crossing my arms across my chest, I rolled my eyes at her. We had been at it for several weeks. Even through the holidays, we met at least twice a week. The turn of the year came, and I was determined to get my voice back, but here we were. All I had accomplished was a small amount of humming so that I could at least agree or disagree. I saw Joy move out of the corner of my eye and looked up from the floor at her.

"We have only been at it for a half hour; you have made progress over these last few months." I sat up and took a piece of paper from the table and a pen and scribbled on it.

"I'm never getting it back am I?" I slid it over to her and she read it. Sighing she looked at me once more.

"These kinds of injuries take time." I huffed again and crossed my arms. "When do you go back to Dr. Francis?" I took the pad and scratched on it and turned it around.

"Wednesday?" Joy asked. I nodded my head.

"Well, I'll be sending her over your progress reports from the last two weeks, and she can discuss with you, what she would like to try next." I felt my shoulders fall. I wanted to be able to talk again.

I had to testify against Solomon in a week and without a voice there was going to be no way to accomplish that.

The ride home was quiet. Despite the music that came through the speakers.

Deafening.

When I walked in the door, Dad was home, sitting on the couch.

"How was your session?" he asked, putting down the paper. I huffed at him. He stood and walked over to me, placing his hands on my shoulders. "You'll get there." He pulled me in, hugging me tightly. I pulled away grabbing the pad of paper that was sitting on the table in the hallway, with a pen.

"How am I supposed to testify against Solomon if I can't talk?" I turned the notepad around and he read it.

"I talked to the prosecutor, and he said that you could write it all down, but someone would have to stand with you and watch you write." I scribbled on the paper again.

"Are you allowed to stand with me?"

"No. It has to be someone of the court." I dropped my hands. For a moment I stood there staring down the hallway into the kitchen. I felt a hand on my foot and my body froze to the spot. Dad reached out and squeezed my shoulder, allowing my mind to separate the feeling and come back to the moment.

"Are you okay?" he asked. I nodded my head and picked up the paper again.

"I miss Jake." I scribbled. He read it quickly and pulled me back into a tight hug.

"Me too, sweetheart." He kissed the top of my head. A knock at the door broke the embrace and he walked around me to answer. I put my keys in the bowl on the hallway table.

"Hi Meg," Dad said. He stepped aside and she walked in.

"Hi, Mr. Twain." I smiled when I saw her. Our visits were always something that made me happy now that I wasn't going to school anymore.

After everything that happened, without being able to speak, Dad and I decided that the best thing for me to do was to continue my studies from home, until things settled down a little bit. I was unnerved when he originally presented the idea as I wasn't keen on staying home by myself. When he had mentioned it I wanted to beg him to let me go back to school, but he assured me that everything was going to be okay. He ended up working remotely and staying home with me every day. When he left the house, I would go with him. It was just recently that I had begun to drive myself again. Leaving the house only to go to my therapy sessions. At first he was driving me, but I wanted to regain control of my life, even knowing I would never be the same again.

A small step towards finding myself once more.

"Isabel?" I broke from my thoughts and found Meg and Dad staring at me.

"What is it?" Meg asked. I shook my head and took her hand. I led her up the stairs to my room.

As I shut the door, she flopped down on my bed, and I did the same. We laid there staring up at the ceiling.

"CJ's been asking about you." I turned my head to look at her. The question in my eyes. "He's just worried. One day you were there the next day you were gone and then you didn't come back." I blinked at her, before sitting up and grabbing another notepad from my bedside table.

"What does he know?" I showed it to her.

"He just knows that you are doing remote learning for now."

"What has he been asking?" I scribbled.

"Just if you are okay, if there is anything he can do, if he can visit you."

"Dad won't let anyone except you, Cecile, and family to see me. He's got the house locked down tighter than Fort Knox. He added a security camera to the living room." She read it.

"I just keep telling him that you will be back before too long and that you are okay. It seems to settle him, but usually only for a few weeks." I dropped the notepad into my lap again and fell back on to the bed. Looking up at the ceiling I could feel tears beginning to well in my eyes. I wanted nothing more than to go back to my old life.

When I had my voice.

When I was going to school.

When I had my brother.

If I had never walked into that building that day and saw the things I had seen then none of this would have ever happened. I would just be a normal girl living a normal teenage life, but instead, my life was anything but ordinary. Her fingers intertwined with mine and I looked at her.

"Things are going to get better and no matter what happens I will always be here for you." I nodded my head, and she squeezed my hand tightly. Turning to face the ceiling again we laid there in silence.

It was a little while later that we walked down the stairs, I could hear Dad clambering around in the kitchen. From the hallway, I could see him struggling to grab something from the cabinet as he tried to balance his phone on his shoulder.

"You have known for months who he is and yet you still haven't found him. How can my daughter feel safe knowing the man that assaulted her still walks freely?" I cleared my throat and Dad turned suddenly. His eyes met mine only briefly, before flicking away as he focused on his phone call.

"Well, I want to be updated on everything that you find. I don't care how many leads you have to follow." He was quiet again. He turned his eyes to me again, his hands full of stuff he had pulled from the cabinet. "Isabel, come grab my phone." I walked over and took the phone from his shoulder; the call had ended. I put it on the counter, and he dropped what he had in his hands.

"I'm sorry." He squeezed my shoulder apologetically. I had known for a while now that Soren Cross was not going to be an easy man to find. He was wanted for several other cases as well, just like his brother Solomon. The only difference was Solomon was still behind bars, whereas Soren was roaming free and could return at any moment. The thought of him coming back brought bile to the edge, threatening to release itself, when I gulped hard to force it back down. I looked at Meg, and she wrapped her arms around me.

"I have to get home, but I'll come back and see you this weekend." I nodded against her, and she pulled away.

"It was nice to see you Mr. Twain."

"Meg, always a pleasure. Tell your folks I said hello."

"Will do." I walked her to the front door. Opening it she turned to me and took my hands in hers, squeezing them tightly.

"If you need anything text me okay." I nodded my head, and she pulled me in for another hug.

I watched her back out the driveway and drive down the road. The chilled air nipped at me as it blew in from across the field and I closed my eyes. I could see him.

Jake.

That day on the boat, those last moments before being swept into the water, never to see him again. I felt my chest shake as a sob arose. I thought of that moment a lot; the moment the light left his eyes. I looked up into the sky.

A silent prayer reaching beyond our plane of existence.

"I hope you are watching. Because I'm still down here fighting, like you taught me."

Dashing away the few tears that had fallen, I took a shaky breath before closing the door.

CHAPTER 6

I sat in Dr. Francis's office, patiently waiting while Dad was texting. I knocked my
foot against the seat, the sound echoing loudly
through the room. Dad brought his eyes to mine,
and I nudged my chin towards his phone.

"I'm just texting your Uncle Ben." I formed a
heart with my hands, a smile spreading on my face.
"I'll tell him that you love him." He looked back
down at his phone and began to tap away again.

When the door opened, Dad stood, putting his phone in his back pocket.

"Mr. Twain. Isabel," Dr. Francis said, shaking each of us by the hand. "How are you feeling today?" She pulled a flashlight out of her pocket and reached for a wooden popsicle stick from one of the jars. Turning her head to me I tilted my head from side to side.

"So, so?" I nodded.

"Well let's take a look here." I opened my mouth, and the terrible taste of the stick touched my tongue drawing a groan from my throat. She pulled the stick out and felt up and down the sides of my neck. She backed up looking at me perplexed and then turned to Dad.

"Have you read any of the reports from speech therapy?" Dr. Francis asked.

"No, I haven't seen anything from them," Dad replied.

"Has she been speaking at all at home?"

"No, she can hum a little, but no words yet."
Dr. Francis looked at me, and her eyes had concern
deeply rooted in them. I held my hands up as I
shrugged.

"Everything has healed nicely." She sighed. "Injuries as severe as these take time. I was hoping
with how well things were going that you would
have some vocal ability."

"What does that mean, since she hasn't?" She
dropped her head and put her hands in her pockets as she turned to Dad again. She looked up at
him.

"It could be psychological, or." She stopped and
glanced at me. "Permanent." I felt the air rush out
of my lungs as the word echoed in the air around
me.

Permanent?

I felt my chest begin to heave and she quickly
produced a box of Kleenex. Taking several, I wiped
the tears from my eyes and blew my nose. Dad got

to his feet and was quickly by my side, one arm around me.

"Is there anything else that can be done?"

"I would recommend getting her into some sort of therapy aside from speech therapy. If we can get to the root of the problem mentally, she still has a chance of getting her voice back."

"And if not?" She sighed heavily as she reached out and took my hand, squeezing it gently. She looked into my eyes.

"We will cross that bridge when we get to it." A sad smile appeared in the corner of her lips before she let go of my hand. Dad pulled my head close to him and planted a soft kiss on my temple.

"You aren't done yet," he whispered.

"I'll send over a referral to a therapist, if you would like," Dr. Francis said. Dad pulled away and looked at me.

"Do you want to see someone new?" I would rather just stick with Courtney, even though I never got through the abduction with her. Everything had gotten out of control. The last time I saw her was through video chat when Jake and I were with Uncle Ben. I shook my head.

"Do you want to go back to Courtney?" I nodded my head. Dad turned to Dr. Francis.

"Thank you, but Isabel has a therapist, she just hasn't been to see her in a while. I can call and make the appointment today."

"Very good, give her my card, so that we can stay in touch about Isabel's improvement," she said as she handed him a card.

"I will, thank you, doctor."

"I'll schedule to see you again in about a month, so we can see if you've made any progress." She looked at me and smiled slightly. I nodded, then she disappeared out into the hallway. Dad hugged me again.

"Come on, let's get you home." I nodded and hopped down from the table.

When we got home, we sat in the living room. Dad had the news on, but my mind was elsewhere.

I stood from the couch and headed toward the stairs.

"Where you going?" I pointed upstairs, putting my hands together and leaning my head on them. I was going to lay down for a little while.

"I'll come get you when dinner is ready." I nodded and headed up.

In the hallway, I sat on the floor, across from Jake's room, the bag still sitting where I had left it. Dad had seen it there but had never tried to move it. There had been countless times since Jake went missing that he would find me sitting right here, staring at it.

It almost seemed a little morbid. Sitting in the hallway, staring at my dead brother's bag instead of putting it in his room.

"You could always put it in the room, you know." I turned my head as it rested against the wall, and he was sitting next to me.

"I'm not ready," I said as a tear slipped down my face.

"It's been eight months. It won't be easy, but you have to do it."

"Why?"

"Because it's how you start moving forward."

"Maybe I don't want to."

"That's the funny thing about living, you always move forward, whether you want to or not." He ran his hand over the top of my head, stopping behind my neck.

"I miss you."

"I miss you too, kid."

I opened my eyes, still leaning against the wall. Turning my head, it was no surprise that Jake wasn't sitting there with me. Just another moment where he came to visit me. He didn't seem to appear much before, but lately he was coming around more often. I welcomed his visits although waking up alone, broke my heart every time. I wiped away the tear from my eye and stood up. Grabbing the straps of the bag, I picked it up and gently pushed the door open.

The room was dark, only a slice of light entered, and I tossed the bag on the floor, before pulling the door shut again.

My legs shook.

Lungs rattling.

Tears rising.

My knees crashed to the floor.

How could something so simple hold so much weight?

A finality that I couldn't process.

"Isabel?" Dad yelled. His footsteps were quick as he came up the stairs. He got on his knees next to me and pulled me against him, my hand falling from Jake's door. Wrapping my arms around him I sobbed as he held me tightly.

"I know, baby. I miss him too."

CHAPTER 7

"Isabel, it's nice to see you again," Courtney said, as she led me into her office. She took a seat at her black metal desk and extended her hand towards a chair.

I sat down.

Dread filling me as I remembered the last time I had been there.

Jake and I had come together.

Now I was alone.

Her fingers tapped the keyboard, staring intently at the screen before regarding me silently.

She pushed a legal pad and pen towards me gently and offered a soft smile. "Your Dad told me a little bit about what was going on when he called, he mentioned that we would need this." I looked down at the legal pad, my only form of communication. I felt my cheeks burn red with embarrassment, as I picked up the pen.

"Tell me a little bit about what's been going on. I haven't seen you in a while." I began to write.

"Did my Dad mention Jake?" I spun it around and she looked at it before nodding her head solemnly.

"He did. I'm so sorry; you must be having a tough time without him." I nodded my head and then turned the paper back towards me. Soft tears began to run down my cheeks, and she passed me a box of tissues.

"Where would you like to begin?" she asked softly. I picked up the pen when everything fell down on top of me.

The heaviness in my chest became too much and the pen fell from my hand. Covering my mouth as the pressure built up in my eyes.

"It's okay. This is perfectly okay. You take as much time as you need." I nodded my head softly, letting the tears soak my face.

After a while I finally settled down.

"Would you like to continue?" Courtney asked. I rubbed my eyes with the sleeve of my jacket and nodded. Taking the pen, I touched it to the paper and stared at the blank page for a minute. I had no idea where to begin, so much had happened, and we never even got through what had originally brought us here.

"You start where you feel the most comfortable." Her voice was encouraging. Sighing heavily, I scratched across the page.

"Jake died."

Courtney nodded slowly. "Do you want to talk about what happened to him?"

I wrote again.

"It was my fault."

"Why?"

My hand shook as I scribbled.

"I went with bad people to save my family. He followed me. He died because he tried to protect me." I turned the paper around, and she glanced at it. A shaky sigh escaped her.

"Are these the same people from before? When you and your friends were taken?" I nodded. That moment came back to me like a tidal wave.

Jake.

The cliff.

The gunman.

Turning.

The gunshot.

It echoed in the back of my mind, and I squeezed my eyes shut.

"You said you went with them to save your friends and family. What do you mean?" Courtney's voice brought me back to the present and I turned the paper towards me again.

"It's my fault they are involved. I was promised that if I gave myself up then they would be spared." She read my words. Reaching across the desk she held her hands out. I looked at them and then back at her as she nodded. Slowly, I reached, letting our hands touch. Hers felt warm against my cold skin, she squeezed firmly, keeping her eyes locked with mine.

"You are not at fault. You cannot change what other people decide to do or how they react to a situation. They drove this into motion and unfortunately, you and your loved ones became caught up in it. You." She stopped, emphasizing. "Are. Not. At fault for other people's actions." I nodded as a stray tear slid down my cheek.

After our session, I got into my car and started the engine. As it came to life, I immediately felt overwhelmed.

A panic attack impending.

Inevitable.

Feeling the thundering in my chest, I immediately fished out the hidden inhaler in the center console. Popping the cap, I put it between my lips and took two large puffs. My hands shook as I put the cap back on, my chest settling, but my mind still unraveling.

I needed to get home.

I had to get out of the open.

With trembling hands I reached for the steering wheel, putting the car in gear. Reversing out of my parking spot I began the drive home.

Driving down the road, light dustings of snow remained on the fields as I passed by. The road was wet from being warmed throughout the day, melting the delicate flakes that had powdered it this morning. My mind focused on the road ahead, pushing back all of the emotions and thoughts from my session with Courtney.

As the house came into view, it was evident immediately that Dad's truck was missing from the driveway. I felt an overwhelming sense of dread as I pulled in. As the car came to a stop, I pulled my phone from my pocket and dialed his number.

"Isabel, are you okay?" I hummed into the phone.

"I didn't expect you to be home so soon, I headed up to grab some stuff from work. I'll be home as soon as I can, lock the door and stay in your room." I hummed again that I understood.

"I love you." I made a kissy sound with my lips, letting him know I loved him too and then hung up the phone.

Inside, I did as I was told, I locked the doors and made sure the back door was locked as well, before going upstairs to my room.

Sitting in bed, I was looking at the homework assignments that had to be finished by Friday.

There were several essays that I needed to write, and it was already Thursday. I dropped my head back against the wall and looked up at the ceiling. My entire session with Courtney playing over in my head, how I just sat there and cried most of the time, and she let me. I could feel a headache coming on. I closed my laptop harder than I intended. Grabbing my phone from beside my leg, the screen lit up, the selfie Jake had taken of us at Keehi was my lock screen.

I stared at his face in the photo.

I was angry.

But I knew deep down, I was angry with myself.

He should never have been there.

He stepped in.

Instead of just letting me do what I had to.

He died because of me.

I stood up with the phone in hand and walked out into the hallway. Stopping in front of his door.

"That's the funny thing about living, you always move forward, whether you want to or not." His words from my dream playing over in my head. With a heavy sigh, I grabbed the knob and pushed the door open, stepping inside.

The hinges squeaked as I closed it to a crack behind me.

The minute I broke the threshold, I felt as though I was betraying his trust. Even though he wasn't here, it still felt wrong. This was his private room, his domain and I was entering without his permission, well without his physical permission. The room was left as though he had just jumped out of bed that morning and left for work.

The bed was unmade.

Drawers were left open.

Clothes hanging out.

Closet door open.

Somehow his cologne still lingered in the air.

A basket of unwashed clothes, by the dresser.

Walking over to his bed I noticed on the night-stand beside the lamp, was a family picture. I picked it up gingerly and studied it. I couldn't have been older than five. Jake and I sat on a blanket with our parents, having a picnic. I remembered the floral; lace collared dress my mom had put on me that day.

As new tears began to rise, I put the photo back. There was a low hum throughout the house, and it felt as though everything had stopped.

Reaching out I turned on Jake's lamp, nothing happened. I clicked it again, and once more it failed to illuminate. I heard the wind outside the window. "*It must have knocked the power out.*" I thought. The silence in the house was almost more than I could tolerate.

The quiet was quickly splintered by the shrill ringing of my phone, making me jump. I grabbed it from my pocket. Dad's name lit up on the screen. I quickly answered it and hummed into the phone.

"Isabel. He's in the house." His voice was low and desperate as though he couldn't breathe. In the background I could hear the roar of the engine of his truck as though he were flying down the road. I felt my heart pounding in my chest at his words.

I heard the squeak of the door as it slowly opened.

My eyes slowly gravitated towards the sound.

There he stood.

Dark eyes.

Sinister smile.

My phone fell from my hand and clattered on the floor.

"Isabel?" I could hear Dad calling me, urgency rising from his voice. I didn't break eye contact with Soren. I stood frozen in fear as my heart palpitated in my chest, my thoughts running wild, trying to find an escape.

I stumbled back, but he was faster.

Hands grabbed me.

Forcing me down onto the bed.

I struggled.

Kicking.

Hitting.

Heart hammering.

He laughed as he ripped at my shirt.

Pain and fear collided.

My shoulder burned from the tear, but I barely registered it.

Desperation guided my hands. I grabbed the lamp on the nightstand and swung. The glass shattered against his head. He howled, falling to his knees. I scrambled for the edge of the bed, then froze as his hand snatched my ankle, yanking me back.

All of the air in me rushed out as I hit the floor.

Memories of our first meeting flashed violently.

The door.

The sound of glass shattering.

My legs scraping against the ground.

Desperate.

Every nerve screamed.

He turned me over, his hands around my throat. I gasped, fighting for air.

His grip was iron.

His eyes wild.

My fingers slid across the floor, desperate for anything.

Anything.

To survive.

My fingers hit something hard under Jake's bed. There was a handle, and I grabbed it. Before I saw it, I was fully aware of what it was. Without hesitation, I pulled it out, my finger finding the trigger and pointing it at him. For a moment, a flash of what looked like fear appeared on his face.

Training the barrel on his face.

"Don't put your finger near the trigger until you are ready, line up your shot and fire." Jake's words echoed in my head. It was in that very moment when my finger squeezed the trigger, deep down I felt whatever sliver of my innocence, of my child-hood that I desperately clung to...

Vanish.

What fragile shards of who I was before being abducted, losing my brother, and being raped, no longer existed, dissipating like the smoke that curled from the barrel.

Into the void that was now my life.

The moment I pulled that trigger....

I became a killer.

The gun recoiled, forcing my shoulders into the floor.

The shot landed between his eyes.

The impact threw him backward, and warmth splattered across my face.

Thud.

"Isabel! Isabel can you hear me?" I could hear Dad's distress as he called out on the phone, breaking the silence, sending tremors through my heart. The sticky warm droplets trailed slowly down my face, making my skin crawl. My hands trembled as I dropped the gun to the floor.

A thick puddle of blood pooled towards me from Soren's lifeless body, causing me to kick against the floor, pushing myself away. My eyes were only able to move away from the blood when the back of my head hit an open drawer from the dresser with a loud crack.

I scrambled to my feet, using the dresser to aid me. I could still hear Dad desperately calling out to me.

"Isabel?"

Click.

It was the phone call ending that jolted me from my stupor, sending panic coursing through my veins. I grabbed the gun and dashed out the door and went back to my room. My black hoodie was draped over the end of the bed. Grabbing it I scrambled into it, before proceeding to the window. Jake's truck was the fastest way for me to get out of here; Dad would track my car in minutes.

Quickly I made my way over to the edge of the roof, throwing the gun to the ground below, before slowly easing myself over the side. Clumsily and in typical fashion, I slipped falling to the ground. My legs buckling as I landed, sending me down hard onto my right arm. A groan escaped me as I grabbed my shoulder and rolled over to catch my breath.

Looking up at the roof above me I realized that it was a bit farther than I had originally anticipated.

Sirens in the distance grabbed my attention.

Getting to my feet, I ignored the pain I felt and grabbed the gun as I raced towards Jake's truck.

Jumping in I pulled open the glove compartment desperately fumbling for the spare key as papers fell onto the floor and seat.

Finding it, I shoved it in the ignition.

It gurgled a little bit.

Slow to start.

My heart began to pound until it roared to life.

Putting it in drive, I floored it.

I could feel the tires grinding up the yard as I drove through the snow dusted grass, toward the road. Turning the wheel hard as the truck slid on the icy asphalt.

I drove away from town.

Pedal to the floor.

Engine groaning.

Looking in the rear view, I felt a breath of relief exhale from my lungs as I didn't see lights coming up the road. My heart pounding as the last few moments replayed in my head.

As I saw the first lights far down, turning onto the road, I turned into an intersection, running the stop sign. An oncoming pickup slammed on their brakes to avoid me, forcing them to slide. They slammed on the horn. Ignoring the driver as he flipped me off, I pushed the gas pedal down as far as it would go.

The engine thundered as I began heading west.

I reached over and sifted through the papers that had fallen on the seat, looking for a map.

Something.

My phone was still on the floor of Jake's bedroom, back at the house and I had no intention to retrieve it. I glanced over and saw a menu in the pile and grabbed it. I held it up; it was a Hodge's Hoagies menu from Nashville. We used to go there at least once a month before mom died. I had no idea where I was going but, I knew Nashville like the back of my hand. I jumped on the highway and headed towards Charlottesville.

As I merged on to the highway, my heart began to calm down slightly, as I kept a close eye out for any police. I looked in the mirror, and looking back at me with red eyes and a blood-stained face was a murderer.

I killed him.

The word carved itself into me: murderer.

A horn blasted beside me, snapping me back into the present. My tires drifted too close to the line as I yanked the wheel straight. My hands were numb on the steering wheel, my muscles trembling as the adrenaline drained away.

Leaving me exhausted.

I took a deep breath, forcing myself to keep my focus on the road ahead of me.

CHAPTER 8

I was barely able to keep myself awake when I pulled into the Greyhound station in Charlottesville. There was only one problem, I didn't have money to purchase a ticket. I lazily started sifting through the truck, seeing if I could find anything. Even if it were just enough to get me out of here. I found some change and a few dollars in the pile on the passenger seat. Picking up the middle seat, there was an envelope in the hidden compartment. Opening it I found three hundred dollars. Sighing heavily, I sat with the money in my hand. I felt bad taking it, but I would pay it back as soon as I could. The thought made my chest feel heavy.

Who would I pay it back to now?

Even still, the thought of taking money he had been saving made me feel terrible. Tears pricked my eyes at the thought.

He should be here.

I glanced up at the mirror; my eyes reddened from the onslaught of tears.

The reason he wasn't.

Sirens broke me from my thoughts, and I slid down in the seat. Looking in the mirrors for the flashing red and blue lights I feared were chasing me. In my reflection, I noticed dried blood droplets on my face. Taking my sleeve, I quickly began to scrub them off. The sound of Soren's body hitting the floor echoed in my skull. The sound made me scrub my face harder, trying to scrub away the blood and the memory. I squeezed my eyes shut as tears threatened to fall.

I didn't have time to sit here and cry.

Getting out of the truck, I stuffed the money and the menu in my pocket, leaving the keys in the ignition and the gun on the passenger seat, half-buried under the glove compartment's spilled contents. I pulled the hood over my head and headed inside the building.

"How can I help you today miss?" He was a kindly old man, with glasses sitting on the bridge of his nose. He squinted at me quizzically as I looked around for something to write on. Finding a pen, I pulled the menu from my pocket and scribbled on it.

"One way to San Francisco please." I turned the notepad around and he read it quickly, before tapping away on his keyboard.

"The next bus leaves in thirty minutes. Can I get your name dear?" He looked at me kindly.

"Isabel Twain." I turned it around and he entered it into the computer.

"Alright, Isabel, your total today is going to be two-eighty-five." I handed him three hundred dollars in cash, and he took it gently from me. He went back to the keyboard, and I heard the drawer on the other side pop open as he put the cash in and handed me back fifteen dollars change. I added it to the additional three dollars and seventy-two cents in my pocket. There was a printing sound, and he turned around quickly, before returning with my ticket. He grabbed something from the side of his desk and my heart froze, fearing that he was alerting the authorities. He gently reached over the counter, handing me two documents.

"Here is your ticket and a map. You are going to be on the Endeavor line so that is the green route, you will be able to see the stops you'll make along the way." I nodded my head at him in thanks as I gently took the papers from his hand. Heading outside, I wandered off near a lamp so I could see what the map showed.

Just as I figured the bus would run right through Nashville and make a stop. That's where I would get off. If the authorities checked the bus station they would see that I got on a bus to California. Dad might think that I went back in hopes of getting to Hawaii to find Jake, as I had never truly given up, that he was alive somewhere. As long as I got ahead, even if they do discover that I got off in Nashville, the trail would run cold as soon as they arrived. I knew that city like the back of my hand and could survive there for as long as I needed to.

I boarded the bus, my legs shaking with every step I took and selected a seat towards the back. Hidden in the shadows I slouched down, anxiety coursing through my veins as I willed the bus to move. As I stared out the window, impatiently waiting the decompression of the doors, my mind wandered back to what had happened.

Soren was there.I shot him.I killed him.

Tears welled in my eyes, I knew I would never be the girl I used to be, but to commit murder. That was not on my sophomore year bingo card. I put my hand over my mouth as the tears started to flow, silencing myself, my fingers were cold, and my hand was shaking. His face became as clear as day. Soren, as horrible and vile as he was, should be dead, but not by my own hands. The bus lurched forward, and I saw my reflection in the window as the light of the evening sun flashed in.

For a second, I saw the girl I used to be.

A loving family.

A cheerful home.

A happy life.

Then she was erased, as the lights faded in the wake of the buses departure.

Past the flicker, blue tear-ridden eyes staring back at me.

The person I had become.

Eighteen months was all it took for who I was before to disappear.

Forever.

As the bus went on, a digital sign above lit up with the name Lynchburg. My heart began to pound as I thought about my Dad who had been there just this afternoon. He had to have gone home, but what if he hadn't?

I made myself smaller still in my seat.

Two police cruisers waited at the depot. My heart began to palpitate as I saw them waiting for the bus to come in.

The bus stopped and the doors opened.

The driver acknowledged the officers as I watched them step up to the door from the window. Over the hum of the engine, I couldn't hear what the officer was saying. The driver shook his head, and my heart fell into my stomach when they began walking away. They stood by the depot door and checked the tickets of the five people who were coming out to get on.

After they checked the last ticket, one turned his head, speaking into his radio, while the other

tipped his hat towards the bus. The driver nodded, closed the doors and the bus began to move
once more. I felt a shallow sigh of relief escape me
as we went by them, keeping my head low so they
wouldn't see me. The PA came to life with a static
crackle.

"Good evening everyone. Sorry for the delay,
settle in we will be arriving in Roanoke in about
an hour." The PA crackled out.

My heart settled a bit as the bus got further away
eventually reaching Roanoke, Max Meadows, and
Knoxville. Looking at my ticket, my transfer was
in Nashville, which was the perfect spot for me to
split off.

Where I intended to vanish.

CHAPTER 9

I spent the majority of the ride staring out the window. The last hours looped on repeat in my mind. The desire to sleep was becoming more desperate, but my eyes couldn't stay closed, no matter how heavy.

My hands shook in my lap.

That last flicker in Soren's face.

I squeezed my eyes shut.

The shock. The fear. The gunshot. The body hitting the floor.

His blood was on my hands.

His wicked smile from our first encounter popped up behind my eyes.

Opening them again, I looked at the window and saw my reflection.

The person looking back at me was someone I didn't recognize.

Dim eyes, once so bright.

A mouth that no longer remembered how to smile.

I shoved myself farther into my seat and rested my head against the cool window.

My thoughts spiraling.

I never knew why the police were at the depot in Lynchburg. I only knew the sight of them wouldn't leave me. They hadn't been looking for me. They *had* looked at the bus.

My chest tightened.

What if they had already been close? What if Dad had gotten there faster than I thought?

What if the driver already knew?

As the bus pulled into the Nashville depot, it hissed as it came to a stop.

The PA crackled to life.

"For anyone traveling onward from here, your next bus should be leaving in the next twenty to forty minutes. For those of you who have reached your destination, welcome to Nashville. Travel safe."

As the PA clicked off, people began to rise from their seats, grabbing bags from the overhead rack. I stood slowly, trying to get the feeling back in my legs.

As the crowd shuffled out in a single file line I kept my eyes to the floor, trying to blend in. The movement was slow, and anxiety was building in my chest.

I felt trapped.

The group was moving too slowly.

I couldn't run or push by, that would make me look suspicious.

As we slowly reached the front, I stepped aside and pulled out the map and wrote on it with the pen I had taken from the bus depot.

"Thank you for getting us here, safely." I showed it to him, and he gruffly read it before peering up at me.

I felt the bruises on my neck burning, as I had my head covered with my hood, knowing he could see them.

See me.

"You alright?" He asked quietly.

I nodded my head.

"You in trouble?"

I shook my head no. He sighed heavily. I cast my eyes to the ground and listened to the shuffling of the people getting off the bus behind me.

"Do you need help?" I looked up at him and shook my head no. I scribbled on the map quickly.

"Have a nice night." He nodded at me, and I got back into the line to get off.

It was just nearing three in the morning, when I stepped off the bus. A gentle layer of snow, crunching under my shoes. The trip had taken just under twelve hours, and a yawn escaped me. I hadn't slept at all. The frigid air split across my face, cutting through my hoodie as I left the warmth.

Pulling my hood tighter, I broke off from the group, stuffing my hands in my pockets as I casually walked off into the night.

I looked back briefly, the driver watching me through the window.

No one else seemed to pay me any mind. Which was exactly what I was hoping for.

As I walked I kept my head low, trying not to attract attention, while also keeping the wind from my face as the bitter cold swirled around me. I pulled my hands from my pockets and wrapped them around me as I walked. The sloshy snow seeping into my shoes with every step, making my feet freeze.

It seemed like an eternity before I reached the familiar landmark, finding myself walking through Centennial Park. By day one of Nashville's notorious tourist attractions, by night it was a hub for those who had nowhere else to go.

In the stillness I could hear coughing coming from the Parthenon, others who sought refuge there from the wintry night.

My eyes grew heavy.

Locating a secluded grove near the pond, surrounded by bushes, I made myself a snug spot in the snow-covered dirt. Curling my legs close, I rested my head on my arms. As the day crashed around in my mind, I felt the hot tears streaming down my icy skin. My chest heaved with sadness and exhaustion.

Eighteen dollars.

No voice.

No name that could save me.

I killed a man and was now going to have to spend my days on the run.

A wracked sob came forward.

Nothing came.

Just breath.

Just cold.

Only the sound of what was left of me breaking in silence.

CHAPTER 10

Awakened by the sound of distant laughter, I opened my eyes.

Streams of light filtering through the branches of the trees above me.

My body shook with cold.

Fresh powdery snow blanketing me.

I sat up.

My long blonde hair was a tangled mess, matted with leaves and grit from the night. I began to brush off the snow as the bitter cold nipped at my fingers. I felt dirty as I got to my knees, glancing to see if anyone would see me leave. With the coast clear I stood and stepped out of my little hiding spot and stretched as the sunlight cast a dim warmth on my face.

"Mommy, why is that girl dirty?" The small voice startled me, and I turned suddenly. My cheeks flushed as I turned my head to see a small girl pointing at me with her mitted hands. Her mother quickly grabbed her arm and put it down, kneeling beside her.

"We don't point at people." She looked at me for a minute, and I could tell that her motherly instinct was pulling for her to do something.

"Are you okay?" she asked. I felt tears welling in my eyes and nodded my head. She regarded me silently for a moment, before standing up.

"Let's go," she sighed heavily. She picked up the child and walked off, disappearing around the bend.

The tears that threatened at the corners of my eyes began to fall, when I looked down and realized how filthy I was. It had been a long night, and I still couldn't wrap my head around what had transpired in my brother's bedroom. I closed my eyes and the moment the bullet crashed into Soren's face, illuminated. I squeezed my eyes tighter willing it to go away when I found myself, backing up bracing against a tree as a breathing fit began.

Lying down I pulled myself back into the cover of the bushes, desperately gasping for air.

I patted my pockets.

No inhaler.

These attacks came far more frequently than before, and I always had an inhaler on hand.

Except this time.

Turning my face into the snow, letting the chill soothe my burning skin, I let the attack spread as I attempted to ground myself to something, anything that would keep me from blacking out.

A wave of panic rushed through me, and I was met with utter darkness and a sense of despair.

My leg felt like it was being pulled.

Soren's vicious smile came to light, forcing me to spring out of the dark and face to face with a homeless man.

He fell back onto his ass as I startled him.

"I'm sorry. I thought you were dead," he said.

I scrambled to my feet and ran out of the bushes; the sun already heavily set behind the city.

Shoelaces licked the back of my legs as I ran.

Exiting the park, I ran down the street.

Unfamiliar faces turning to look at me as the crowd began to thicken.

Turning a corner, I slowed and began to catch my breath.

Another attack lingering within my lungs, threatening to spring forward if I didn't stop. I stepped into the opening of an alleyway and leaned against the brick wall. The cold bricks sending a chill down my spine as condensation fogged heavily from my mouth.

The air was getting crisper by the minute and if I didn't find somewhere warm, I was sure I would freeze to death. Reaching into my pocket, I pulled out the menu for Hodge's. Unfolding it I looked at the address. If anything, I could at least go there and get warm for a little bit. Stepping out of the alleyway I found a street sign. I was only a few blocks away from the address. I began to make my way to Porter Street.

As I walked down the street, the sidewalks became flooded with more people, there was constant eye contact.

Anyone could recognize me.

I had no way of knowing what time it was, but all it would take was a run in with an officer to have me carted off to the big house. There was a grip on my heart as I thought about being picked up.

I was likely wanted for murder by now.

My thoughts ran through everything at lightning speed and then...

Dad.

His voice, calling my name.

The sound of his terror.

I couldn't imagine what it was like for him to hear the things he did.

The altercation that ended with a body hitting the floor in a hard final, brutal thud.

Not knowing who had gone down.

The blast rang in my ears.

Tormenting me.

I forced my thoughts on my steps.

My feet feeling like blocks of ice.

Closer to Broadway, I could see the vast numbers of people hanging around. Turning down Porter, the crowd had doubled. I pulled my hood up over my head, keeping my eyes cast to the ground.

I slipped through the bulk like a phantom.

Eyes searching for the familiar eatery.

Slamming into something hard I stumbled.

The glow of the streetlight slipped away as I stood in the shadows of a dark alley.

A man dusting himself off.

He straightened himself and my eyes met his.

He was clearly inebriated, tripping over his own two feet.

I backed away.

He stepped closer.

The alley was completely empty, aside from the dumpsters that were housed there.

He stumbled.

"Where you going?" he slurred. My heart slammed in my chest.

Like a warning.

Begging me to run.

My eyes darted in a panic.

Looking for a way out.

Spotting a door, I sprinted.

Yanking it open, I ran inside.

"Come back," his voice echoed behind me. I slammed the door shut the click, sending a shiver up my spine. Looking down the hallway, it was dark and there was loud music radiating throughout. There were doors with clearly marked bathroom signs.

My eyes drifted to the wall, I could see older signage, one included the familiar sign of Hodge's Hoagies. Along with it was a framed newspaper clipping, showing the front of the store, renamed, Scarlett's Web. I heard the crashing of a door and froze as the women's bathroom door had swung open.

A small group of women stumbled out, laughing as they held drinks in their hands.

Keeping a safe distance, I followed them.

They entered a giant room, and the layout was one I recognized. Hodge's was now a thriving bar, taking in the overflow of people from Broadway.

The room was packed. Sweat, bodies colliding on the dance floor, drinks spilling everywhere.

Turning my head, I saw a group of people doing body shots in the corner of the bar, a red rope around the table they were partying at. My heartbeat matched the rhythm, coming from the speakers.

Anxiety filled me.

I had no business being in a bar at my age.

It wouldn't be long before someone noticed I was out of place.

I heard the slamming of a door behind me and panic rippled, propelling me into the crowd. Looking for a way out.

Racing through the crowd, the smell of alcohol giving me a high as people flooded the floor. I could feel my feet sticking as I stepped in spilled drinks.

I just wanted to get out.

Stepping up on a short platform, I looked around, standing on my tip toes, looking above the sea of heads, finding the front door. I jumped off the platform and began running towards the exit, weaving in and out of the crowd as best as I could without disturbing their fun.

As I made my way through, a sound pulled me to a sudden stop.

A familiar laugh filtered from the direction of the bar.

It was like that of a phantom.

I turned my head.

He was facing away from me.

His sandy blonde hair was longer.

He wore a black t-shirt and jeans.

He was leaning forward and his head turned as he addressed the person next to him, another man in the same attire.

I would recognize that laugh anywhere.

My heart leapt into my throat as I turned on my heels and rushed over. He was facing the bar again, and an exasperated sigh escaped me as I wrapped my arms around him, hugging him tightly from behind. Burying my face into his back I began to sob with tears of relief.

With an inhale my tears ran cold.

The cologne.

It wasn't Jake's.

He stiffened under my touch, turning around he quickly seized me by the shoulders, holding me away from him. I looked up, realizing that I had been wrong. His hair was dark and long, with a long well-groomed beard to match, he was built and slightly taller than Jake. A faint scar running from above his eyebrow, across and down into his cheek.

A cold chill ran down my spine.For a moment, I thought...That he was.But he wasn't.He wasn't Jake.

But his eyes.

I had seen those eyes before.

Just not on him.

PART TWO

Mike

CHAPTER 11

I tore into the driveway.

Mind reeling.

Chest thundering.

I counted the number of squad cars that surrounded my house. I had followed the last set of lights as they pulled in and I slammed the brakes. Jumping out of the truck I raced past an officer.

"Sir, you can't go in there," he yelled.

"My daughter is in there!"

I ran in the door and up the stairs, shoving through the officers that had gathered on the second floor.

Outside of Jake's room.

I pushed my way to the front as they grabbed at me.

A body, on the floor.

Blood all over the walls and bed.

A bullet hole through the head.

I recognized his face almost immediately, from the cameras in the living room.

It was Soren Cross.

I let them pull me back.

Slamming against the wall of the hallway, tears of relief fell from my eyes as I covered my mouth.

Through the crowd I made out the unmistakable phone that belonged to Isabel.

Isabel.

I raced down the hallway.

"Isabel!" I yelled.

Maybe if she heard me, she would appear.

I pushed her door open.

Bed empty.

Drapes floating on the breeze.

Silence.

"Isabel?"

Where could she be?

She had to be here somewhere.

I stood silent, waiting for something.

Anything.

Steps came down the hallway.

Panic surged through me.

Thoughts began to swirl in my mind.

What if he wasn't working alone?

What if she had been taken again?

I went to the window, looking out.

It was then I realized.

Jake's truck was gone.

"Mike?" I turned to see Chuck, standing in the doorway. "Where is Isabel?"

"I don't know. Jake's truck is gone; she must have taken it."

"We need to find her." I turned my eyes meeting his and my heart fell into my chest. His eyes said everything.

"She's not a murderer, Chuck. He attacked her before, and he came back; this had to be an act of self-defense."

"I know that, Mike, but we still need to talk to her. Also." He stopped for a moment. "If she's not found and returned before trial Solomon will walk free." I felt my eyes widen. That monster was not going to get out and walk after what he did to my kids. There was no way in hell I was going to let that happen.

"How could they just let him out?"

"Isabel is the key witness to his case. If she doesn't show to testify they will let him go free."

"We can't ask them to postpone?"

"They won't be able to."

"I'll get Jake's license plate information for you here in a second." Chuck nodded and disappeared down the hallway. I watched him stop and talk to one of his officers as they stood outside of Jake's room. A set of paramedics with a gurney made their way up the stairs. I walked out of Isabel's room and headed to mine.

I kept all of the important documents in my safe.

Opening it, I quickly found the information for Jake's truck. I walked back into the hallway and handed it to Chuck. He took it from me and turned his head into the radio that was clipped to his shoulder.

"This is Sheriff Beck, I need a BOLO for a nineteen-ninety-eight, Chevy Silverado, black. License plate number Echo, Sierra, Nevada, zero, nine, one, Kilo." I overheard the feedback coming from the radio.

Why hadn't I put a tracker in his truck?

I had one in her car, I never thought.

My thoughts were interrupted as a name came through the static.

"Jake Twain." My heart dropped. Silent claws digging into my heart, thinking about the son that I had lost.

"Isabel Twain, is suspected to be driving the vehicle."

"Is it stolen?"

"No. She's an endangered minor."

"Copy that, sending information to all available units and agencies."

"Copy, over." The radio went silent, and he looked at me.

"We are going to find her, Mike." I nodded my head, and he walked away.

Numbly, I walked down the hallway. The echoes of cameras' flash heightened as the flash lit up the dim hallway.

As I made it to the bottom of the stairs, a ringing in my ears replaced the chaotic exchanges between officers.

Opening the door, I was assaulted by a bright flash.

The media had shown up, and they were looking for comment.

An officer removed the photographer from my immediate area. Looking around my chest tightened, there was nothing I could do, there was no one with me at this moment that would help me. I knew Chuck and his agencies would do their best, but I needed someone who would help me do whatever it took to get my daughter back.

Stepping back into the house and away from the prying eyes of the media, I strode through the house and popped out the back door onto the back porch. Jerking my phone from my back pocket I quickly dialed the number as soon as I found it. The phone rang a few times before the call connected.

"Hello?" The voice on the other end was groggy. I knew he would be sleeping, but this was an emergency.

"Benny." My voice shook as I spoke, followed by a sniffle as I tried to keep the tears at bay.

My daughter was missing.

I had no idea what to do.

No idea who else to call.

My brother was the only person I could think of.

I couldn't call my parents.

Or Jen's.

She couldn't have gotten far, although I had no idea how much time had passed.

If only I had driven faster.

What if she was hurt?

What if she was dying?

My mind was a frenzy, until I heard his voice come through again on the other line.

"Mikey, what is it?"

"It's Isabel."

"What happened?" I heard the urgency in his voice and the bed shuffle as he moved on the other side of the phone.

"She's gone."

"What do you mean gone?" I heard him pulling drawers open.

"Soren Cross is dead, and she's gone."

"How do you know he's dead?"

"There's a crime scene unit cleaning his body up off of Jake's bedroom floor."

"What the hell happened? Where is Isabel?"

"She's run away."

"What do you need me to do?"

"How fast can you get here?" I heard drawers closing on the other end.

"I can be there on the next flight."

"Thank you."

"No need to thank me, we are family. We show up for each other."

"I'll see you soon."

"See you." My chest felt heavy as the call ended and I watched as the coroner came out, pulling the gurney with the black bag that contained Soren Cross's body.

CHAPTER 12

I stayed in a hotel in Richmond that night, as the police had corded off the house. I knew that they would be doing it, but it felt odd, not staying in the house, not knowing where the hell my daughter was. I anxiously awaited by my phone the whole night. The years of training keeping me awake, waiting for something that would indicate her whereabouts. Her phone had been left behind, leaving me no hope of tracking her that way.

As I waited in the baggage claim area, my foot tapped impatiently as I stared down at my phone. It was just a little after twelve-thirty. There had been no word on Isabel and nothing from Chuck about Jake's truck. It was a hand on my shoulder that broke me from my thoughts, and I looked up from the screen and into the deep brown eyes of my little brother.

"Benny." He wrapped his arms around me, and I felt like a broken man.

"You know I'll always be here for you and the kids." He pulled away and regarded me silently. "Have you heard anything?"

"No. Not yet." I saw someone approaching in my peripheral and turned. To my surprise, Sitka and Keone were standing there.

"Mr. Twain." Sitka extended his hand, and I took it. I looked back at Ben.

"What are you guys doing here?"

"Sitka and Keone have been staying with me for a while. There was a storm that damaged their surf shop, and I offered for them to stay with me until the repairs are done. When you called I got up and began packing and when I told them I was leaving, they insisted on coming with me. So here we are."

"Isabel is our friend. We couldn't do much to help Jake, but I told her we would always be there for her." I looked at Sitka and could see the desperation in his eyes.

To help.

To keep his promise to Isabel.

One that I had witnessed in my own son's eyes once. He wanted to do this for Jake. I felt my chest heave, and I had to force the tears away as I thought about him.

"Grab your bags boys, we need to get moving," Ben said. I broke from my thoughts, and they walked over the carousel and grabbed their bags. Returning to us, we headed outside and quickly got into the truck.

As we pulled away the screen on the dash lit up with a phone call.

"It's Chuck." I immediately stabbed at the answer button.

"Chuck?"

"Mike, we found the truck." His voice echoed throughout the cab.

"Where is it?"

"Charlottesville, at the Greyhound Bus depot."

"Did they see Isabel?"

"We got them to show us the security footage. She bought a ticket to San Francisco."

"Can they stop the bus?"

"They are looking to see where the bus has registered, she had a few hops so if they can locate the bus, they were going to send authorities to meet it at its next stop."

"Alright. We are on our way."

"See you soon." I ended the call, and my foot pushed down on the pedal, the engine roaring loudly as the truck lurched ahead, racing to the highway.

"Why would she go to San Francisco? Does she know someone out there?" Ben asked.

"Not that I know of. The only thing ever brought up about San Francisco, is that's where Solomon was arrested."

"Could she be trying to go back?" Sitka asked from the backseat.

"To Hawaii?" Ben replied.

"Yeah."

"Mike?" Ben said. I looked at him and then looked at the two boys in the rearview mirror.

"It's possible."

"Why would she go back?" Ben asked.

"She still thinks Jake could be alive."

"Shit." It came out almost as a whisper.

"After everything that happened after we got back, she kept saying she felt like he was alive and nothing I told her, registered. After what Soren did." I stopped; I didn't want to talk about what Soren had done to her. My grip on the steering wheel tightened as I remembered the phone call that I had received that day. The hospital telling me that my daughter had been brought in.

"What happened?" I had asked.

"You should get here, and we can talk then."

"Is she okay?"

"Mr. Twain."

"Is my daughter alive?" I had interrupted.

"Yes."

"Mike?" I broke from my thoughts and looked at Ben, his concerned eyes on me. Looking down at my hands on the steering wheel I could see that my knuckles had turned white with how hard I was gripping it.

"For the longest time she left his bag outside of his room and I have caught her sitting in the hallway outside of the door, often."

"Didn't you try to send her to therapy? That's unhealthy behavior."

"Yes, she was going back to therapy, especially after what happened. It obviously didn't help because she still sat in that hallway." My mind flicked through the memories I had of the times I would catch her sitting there. Sometimes she would see me coming and leave, thinking that I hadn't seen her. Other times I would have to wake her up because she had fallen asleep.

My poor sweet girl. First she had lost her mother and then lost her first best friend. Jake was always good to her, from the moment we had brought her home from the hospital, he helped with her feedings, changing her diaper, helping picking an outfit for her. He used to parade her around in her stroller and tell anyone who would listen to him that he was proud to be her big brother. The memory brought tears to the corners of my eyes. He was a great kid and an exceptional young man. His death shook the entire family, but it destroyed Isabel. I sighed heavily as I turned the truck onto the highway and the engine roared as I pressed the gas pedal harder.

"Do you want me to drive?" Ben asked. I looked at him, and a small smile creased into the corners of my lips.

"Scared?" I turned my attention back to the road.

"No, but you are under a lot of stress at the moment."

"I'm fine."

"You're not fine." I glanced at him again quickly and could see the concern in his eyes.

"Don't worry little brother, I got this." He held his hands up relenting.

"I'm here, whatever you need." I nodded and turned my focus back to the stretched highway.

Chapter 13

As we arrived at the depot in Charlottesville, it was nearly two in the afternoon, Chuck was waiting for us with another deputy. They were parked next to Jake's truck with the doors opened. Seeing my son's truck wide open and being searched brought a painful sting to my heart.

It had been sitting for months, never started, never moved after I had moved it to the backyard. I couldn't wrap my head around why Isabel would have taken it, instead of her own car. There was an officer taking photos as well as dusting the steering wheel. Parking the truck, I turned and looked at the boys in the back.

"Stay here. Ben you're with me." We got out of the truck and approached Chuck. He walked up and extended his hand to me. We shook briefly before he shook Ben's hand.

"Chuck, this is my brother Ben."

"From Hawaii?"

"Yes, sir, it's nice to meet you in person."

"Just wish it was under better circumstances," he said, shaking Ben's hand. Ben nodded in agreement.

"Did you find anything?" I asked. He opened his mouth to speak.

"Sir." We turned our heads toward the truck as the officer stood back from the door, a gun in his gloved hand. Chuck began taking the steps toward him and put a glove on as he took the gun from him. He studied it before holding it up for me to look at. I sighed heavily as I recognized the customized grip on the gun.

"It's one of Jake's." He nodded and the other officer appeared at his side, holding open a plastic evidence bag. "Where did you find it?"

"It was on the passenger seat, under some stuff from the glove compartment."

"Do you think this is the gun she used, Mike?" I nodded. There was no other excuse for it to be in the truck as I had cleaned it when I parked it in the backyard.

"They'll need to run tests on it, but once the investigation closes, I'll make sure it is returned to you." I nodded.

"Is there anything else?" I had to know if they had reason to believe she was hurt.

I had to know if my daughter was out there...

Alive.

"No."

The word thumped in my head like a heartbeat and relief filled my chest.

Only briefly.

"Have they been able to track Isabel's bus?" Ben asked.

"I should be hearing back shortly." As though they heard us speaking from outside, his cell phone began to ring. He held it up. "That's them now." He turned and walked away as he answered the call. My anxiety was rising as I watched him kicking his foot off the ground as he spoke on the phone.

I felt a hand on my shoulder.

"Don't worry, Mike. We are going to find her," Ben said.

"You don't understand."

"What don't I understand?"

"If she doesn't come back, Solomon will walk free."

"What?"

"Without Jake she's the only one that can testify against him."

"How much time do we have?"

"She's supposed to take the stand Monday."

"That's not a lot of time."

"I asked if we could postpone it, but Chuck says they won't it's been changed enough times."

"Why did she leave to begin with? Was she scared?"

"I'm not sure. All I know is that Soren Cross came back, now he's dead and." I stopped, the words catching in my throat. "She's gone." I looked off into the distance. "I don't even know if she's hurt."

"She's a tough kid, Mike. You heard them. They didn't' find anything else." The tension thickened around us.

I nodded.

"I heard a struggle on the phone and then a gunshot. Isabel shot him." His hand fell from my shoulder, and I turned to look at him.

"Are they trying to say she's a killer?"

"No, they know it was self-defense."

"Then why did she run?" I looked back at Chuck who was still on the phone.

I sighed heavily.

"I don't know."

Chuck finally ended the phone call and walked back over to us, with his eyes cast to the ground.

"What is it?" Ben asked.

"They stopped the bus in El Paso. When officers boarded, they checked the manifest, her name was on it, but she wasn't." I felt my heart drop into my chest. She could be anywhere between here and Texas.

"There has to be someone that saw her." I said as I ran my hand through my hair.

"There was the bus driver from the bus she left on. They reached out to him, and he said that he did see her. "

"Where would she go?" I heard the voice from behind me; I was so caught up in my own thoughts that I never heard the door to the truck open. Sitka was standing next to us now.

"Why did she buy a ticket to San Francisco?" Ben asked. I took a shaky breath.

"I thought maybe she was trying to find a way back to Hawaii, to find Jake."

"But Jake is gone."

"She still thinks he's alive somewhere. She won't accept it."

"But if she isn't going there, then where did she go?"

"I don't know." My eyes met Ben's and there was worry building in his. He would never recover from what happened to Jake and I know that he would never forgive himself. He felt responsible as he was meant to be protecting them when I was unable to.

Leading Isabel to try giving herself up to protect her loved ones.

Costing Jake his life.

"What are the other stops?" Sitka asked. Chuck looked up at him.

"What do you mean?"

"Well, she isn't on the bus and it's in El Paso, that means she had to have gotten off somewhere." Chuck pulled out his phone and called back the number he had just hung up with.

"I need a list of all the stops from here to El Paso, starting with the bus that left Charlottesville." He was quiet for a moment. Pulling a pad of paper and a pen from his pocket he began to jot down quickly, everything he was hearing from the other end.

When he hung up the phone he ripped the piece of paper from the pad and handed it to me. I looked at the list, and I felt the air dissipate from my lungs; the moment I felt Ben's hand grip my shoulder, as he read the list alongside me.

"Nashville," Ben said. I looked up at Chuck and then at Ben.

"Is Nashville significant?" Chuck asked.

"Yes," Ben replied.

"Why would she get off in Nashville?" Chuck asked. I sighed as I put the list in my pocket.

"Isabel was raised in a suburb just outside of Nashville. Mount Juliet," Ben replied.

I began to think about our house there, how Jen and I worked arduously to buy that house so that we could raise our family there. She was six months pregnant with Isabel when the sale went through. She was so happy. Jake was just starting Kindergarten, and he was already in big brother mode, helping Jen set up the nursery after we moved in. I exhaled heavily, putting my hands on my hips and turning my head towards the sky, the evening beginning to settle in above us.

"She's going home."

CHAPTER 14

We stood on the porch just before nine, the night thick and restless. I wanted to be back in the city, searching. Ben had insisted on rest. I hadn't slept in days. The porch light came on, and her small frame shuffled to the door. As it opened she stood cautiously in the entryway, her eyes widening as she spotted us in the light.

"Mikey? Benny?"

"Hi, mom." She stepped back, letting us walk in, hugging both of us as we stepped in, stopping and eyeing the two boys that followed us in.

"Mom, you've seen Sitka and Keone on video chat," Ben said. Her eyes lit up when she suddenly recognized them. She gave each of them a hug as she welcomed them in.

"Boys, it's so nice to finally meet you, come in, come in." She shuffled to the kitchen as we followed her, taking seats at the table.

"Coffee? Water?" She offered.

"I need something stronger, and I think my brother here could use something stronger as well if you have it," Ben said, slapping my shoulder. She nodded and reached into a cabinet in the corner, returning to the table with two rocks glasses and a bottle of brandy.

"Soda for the boys?"

"Thank you ma'am," Sitka said. She went to the fridge and returned with two sodas. She took a seat at the table and folded her hands, eyeing my brother and I curiously. She had questions and I knew that she wasn't going to like the answers.

"Where is my granddaughter?" I knew it. I gently took the bottle of brandy and poured myself a shot, downing it. The burn slowly creeping its way down my throat and into my chest.

Clearing my throat, I looked at her and her eyes left mine and went to Ben, looking for an answer. Her eyes returned to mine, the corners of them creasing with worry.

"Mikey?"

"I don't know." I ran my hands over my face and sighed heavily, Ben, poured himself a shot and then poured me another.

"What happened?"

"She ran away," I replied, picking up the glass and downing another round.

"Why?" I looked at Ben and he nodded.

"The man that attacked her came back."

"No." She clutched her chest, as though she was preparing to hear the worst news to date.

"Yes." I stopped struggling with the words that were about to come next.

I cleared my throat.

"Isabel killed him."

The words collapsed the room. Mom didn't move. Didn't breathe. Just stared at me like the sentence hadn't reached her yet

"Mom, where's Dad?" Ben asked, breaking the silence.

"He's upstairs, sleeping. Do you want me to wake him?"

"No. No, that's fine, we can tell him in the morning."

"Why are you here?" Mom was directing the question to me.

"We have reason to believe that she's here."

"Why would she come here?"

"She bought a bus ticket to San Francisco; they located the bus in El Paso, and she wasn't on it. Nashville was a stop on the route. I think she got off and is somewhere in the city." I cleared my throat.

"She practically grew up in Nashville; she knows it better than most people." I nodded.

"She has to be here somewhere."

"How can your father and I help?"

"We are just here to stay for the night; we are going into the city tomorrow to look for her."

"Your father will go with you."

"We have all the manpower we need between the four of us. What I need for you two to do is stay here in case she gets desperate and comes home." Mom scoffed slightly and waved me off.

"That girl of yours is far from desperate. She has handled every situation thrown at her and come out shining like gold."

"Mostly," I sighed as I rubbed my eyes.

"What do you mean?"

"She's still struggling with Jake's passing."

"You expect her not to?"

"It's not that, it's like she's determined to convince herself that he is alive somewhere."

"Maybe that's how she has decided to cope."

"That's not a healthy way to cope," I sighed.

"No, but it's her way. She's always been a tough little girl." She took my hands in hers, our eyes locking. "Mikey, she has been through so much in the last eighteen months. That's a lot for someone so young." I freed a hand, running it over my face again.

She was right.

Nothing had been easy for Isabel since she lost her mom.

Then I turned around and left her and her brother when they needed me the most.

Tears sprang forward from my eyes, and I couldn't stop them.

"Boys, let me show you the guest room," Ben said. I heard them scoot back from the table and leave the room, as I hid my face, while I cried. I heard mom's chair scoot back and soon felt her arms around me. Hugging me and shushing me gently.

"It's okay, honey," she cooed.

"It's not okay. I'm a terrible father."

"Now, why on earth would you say that?" She challenged.

"They lost their mother, and I took away their home. Then I left them."

"You had your own grief to work through."

"But I should have put them first."

"You made a mistake honey, that's what parents do. We make mistakes and learn from them. There's not a how-to guide when it comes to raising children."

"My mistakes almost cost me Isabel."

My voice cracked.

"And I lost Jake."

The tears came harder when I said his name. "My beautiful boy." Mom hugged me tighter as my body was rocked by the grief I felt in my chest.

In my moment of grief, I thought of Jennifer.

She had been the love of my life from the first time I met her. I knew the very moment her crystal blue eyes met mine that I would marry her and have a family one day.

Here I was, crying in my mother's kitchen.

My wife and son dead.

My daughter missing.

I couldn't even begin to imagine what she would think of me at this moment.

I had let my kids down.

I had let Jen down.

Another wave hit me, and I felt mom's arms tighten around me.

CHAPTER 15

The sun had barely scratched the horizon when I got up. I had a tough time sleeping anyway, even the brandy didn't help. The entire night my mind was flooded with finding Isabel, as well as thoughts of Jake. For years there was never one without the other and now that time had passed, seeing Isabel without him was always haunting. I got up and rubbed my hands over my face, quickly I got around. I was lacing up my boots when Ben walked in, his hair a mess.

"You're up early," he yawned.

"I need to get into the city."

"Well give me a few minutes and I'll get the boys, and we can head down."

"Okay, but please hurry. I want to find her. We only have a few days until Solomon's trial and if she doesn't show he walks. I'll be damned if that bastard walks free after what he and his twisted brother did to her." Ben nodded and strode back out of the room.

When he returned, Sitka and Keone were in tow. They were dressed and ready to go. Sitka was just tying his hair up.

"They were up and going already," Ben said. I looked at them as they stood wearing shorts and hoodies.

"Are you guys going to be warm enough? It's colder here than what you are used to." Sitka looked at Keone, before turning his gaze back to me.

"We are good," Sitka said, nodding his head.

"That's what I like to hear. Now I need you, Benny." He looked down at his attire and nodded.

"Give me ten."

"Five." He nodded and walked off.

As we drove into the city, the streets were empty. It was still pretty early at seven in the morning, and the only people out were those who got up around five in the morning for coffee. Every street we drove down, I scanned silently searching for any sign of Isabel.

"Where are some of her favorite places?"

"Centennial Park, Hodge's Hoagies, other than that I couldn't say. Jen always brought them into the city; I only accompanied them a few times."

"Well let's check the park, it's still pretty early, maybe if she is staying there, she will still be sleeping," Ben said.

"The homeless are abundant at night around there, I don't know if she would go there."

"She might if she felt she had no choice."

"We can go take a quick look." I turned down the next street and headed towards the park.

When we arrived, we walked around. I pulled a picture from my wallet of her, maybe if she had been here someone may have seen her. There were a few people huddled together near the water's edge, washing their hands. Looking around there were others who had packed up their stuff and were preparing to head to the pantries for a hot breakfast. Ben and I walked up to the men washing their hands, the boys staying close behind us.

"Excuse me." The three men looked up at me startled.

"Don't worry we're leaving," one of them said. He was wrapped in a filthy blanket, his pants had holes in them and his brown beanie rested on his head lopsided. He looked as though he had just woken up.

"Please, have you seen this girl?" I held out the picture to the men, and they stared at it intently for a moment. "This is my daughter; she ran away from home, and I believe she may have come here."

"Hey, Brut." The man with the brown beanie yelled. There was a rustle in a nearby bush, and a man poked his head out.

"Yeah?" His body was shielded by the bush.

"These folks are looking for a missing girl." Brut walked out the bushes, zipping up his pants, kicking his leg out, shaking it.

"Is that so?" He walked over and the man with the brown hat, gently took the picture from my hand and held it out for Brut to see. He gently took it from him and studied the picture.

"That's her alright."

"You've seen her?" My heart lifted as he shook his head in confirmation.

"Yes, that's right."

"When? How long ago?" He sighed heavily and scratched his head as he looked at the others.

"She gave him a fright a couple days ago," the man with the brown hat said.

"How so?" Ben asked.

"Well, you see, I found her lying in that bush over there," Brut pointed towards a small grove of trees and some bushes. "I thought she was passed on from this life and I might have startled her when I tried to move her." Ben looked down at his feet and then back up at him.

"Why were you trying to move her?" he asked.

"That's just what we do. If someone doesn't survive the night, we move them somewhere more secluded and alert the police when they do their rounds in the morning." Ben nodded. Brut handed the picture back to me.

"Do you remember which way she went?" Brut threw his head in the opposite direction.

"She headed toward Broadway." I gently put the picture back in my wallet and put it back in my pocket.

"Thank you so much, I can't tell you how much I appreciate your help."

"No problem, mister, we just hope you find your little girl." The others nodded in agreement with him. I nodded in thanks, and we quickly made our way back to the truck.

We drove towards Broadway, scanning again as the streets began to fill with people going about their Sunday shopping. Tourist wouldn't be out as they were all hung over or still passed out drunk from partying all weekend.

"We should pull over, we might have a better chance, if we are in the crowds," Ben suggested.

"I feel like we would miss her," I said.

"What's that other place you mentioned?"

"Hodge's Hoagies."

"We should swing by there and see if she might be hanging out there." I nodded and headed towards Hodge's.

As we pulled up, we parked out front of the familiar building. The front had been redone and the sign above it now said, Scarlett's Web.

"Must have been bought out," Ben said. I looked at the windows; there were neon signs hanging unlit in the windows.

"She wouldn't be here now, it's a bar, they would never let her in." I felt my heart rate quicken. We were at a dead end. I felt Ben's hand on my shoulder.

"It's okay, we are going to find her. We at least know that she is here somewhere in the city."

"It's been really cold out the last few nights, what if she's." I stopped. I couldn't bring myself to say the words out loud. Not after losing Jake. I wasn't willing to imagine even for a minute, despite the horrendous thought raking it's way at the back of my mind, that Isabel was gone.

"She's a smart girl. She survived being lost in the woods for several days. She can manage to find somewhere warm in the city." He was right, she was a smart girl, and she would do whatever it took to survive.

"Should we check the shelters?" Sitka asked from the backseat.

"It wouldn't hurt, maybe she went looking for warmth or food," Ben sighed. I nodded.

"There's a few of them along Broadway, we can check them while we hit the pavement." I killed the engine on the truck and stepped out of its warmth into the cold embrace of the morning. Ben stepped out and I heard his zippo clink as he lit a cigarette. I looked over at him across the hood.

"Those things will kill you," I said. He smiled slightly as he exhaled.

"There's worse things out there that have already tried." I cocked a smile at him briefly. If there was anyone who understood the perils of war, it was me and Ben. Growing up I never imagined that he would follow me into the military. He was Jake's age when he joined up. Jake was just starting middle school at the time. There was a ten-year age gap between us.

He probably didn't know it, but I worried about him a lot.

Just like Jake had always worried about Isabel.

"We should start canvasing Broadway, there's already a lot of people out, and if she is running around out there, she would stay inside the crowds." Ben nodded and we began walking down Twelfth, toward Broadway, my eyes dodging amongst faces as we walked, taking zero chances of missing her.

It was near noon when my frustration had reached a peak. We had been on the ground looking for nearly three hours with not a single sighting. Agitated, I threw my back against a wall.

"It's still early." Ben said.

"It's noon, most of the people have already headed home," I said lowly. The air held and icier touch than it had previously in the morning. My fingers had lost feeling a long time ago, I only ignored it because I was so focused on finding Isabel. Ben put his hand on my shoulder and leaned against the wall next to me.

"We should take a break. Get back to the house and warm up. These kids are looking a little blue." I turned my attention to Sitka and Keone, completely forgetting that they had never been to an area like this before. They were both wearing hoodies, but those weren't nearly enough for the weather as it changed.

"We can stay. We need to find Isabel," Keone said.

"We can come back and look later," Ben said.

"No. Really, we can keep going," Sitka encouraged. Ben looked at me, and I shook my head.

"Ben's right, we need to go back and warm up. Staying out here and freezing won't do us any good in finding her." Relenting the boys nodded and we began to make the long trek back down Broadway towards the bar, where we had left the truck.

As we walked the silence that surrounded us was quickly shattered by the sound of sirens.

Echoing from nearby.

We stopped where we stood, and an icy hand gripped my heart.

It could be anything.

My heart pounded.

It could be...

Isabel.

My feet began pounding the pavement.

Panic radiated through my body.

"Mike!" He yelled after me. As I ran I heard their footsteps catching up behind me. I rounded the corner to Twelfth and stopped suddenly. The street was empty.

There was no ambulance.

No urgency.

Just silence.

They caught up to me, and we stood staring down the road.

"Mike, what is it?" Ben asked again.

I was losing my mind.

That's what was happening.

"I thought I heard something."

I tried to push it away.

But something still clawed at me.

Warning me of a connection.

We began walking towards Porter.

I stopped dead when I saw it and Ben put his hand on my shoulder and squeezed it tightly.

"Don't lose your head, Mikey."

I didn't move.

Didn't speak.

All I could do was stare at the smeared blood on the snowy sidewalk, droplets leading the way we were heading.

"Let's go." I followed the trail closely and sure enough it turned down towards the bar where we had left the truck. Down the road, near the truck I could see the tail end of an ambulance driving the opposite direction. I raced towards the bar, my heart pounding.

When we reached the bar, a young man was hurriedly coming out. I walked up to him and when he turned, his eyes met mine.

My heart stopped.

If it weren't for his dark hair, beard, the scar on his face, height, and large build I would have sworn it was my son. He looked irritated as we had stopped him from doing whatever he was doing as he seemed to be in a hurry. I quickly pulled the picture of Isabel out.

"Have you seen this girl?" I asked as I held the picture out. He took it from me and studied it for a minute.

Without warning, he landed a punch to my face. Blood began rushing from my nose as I leaned over.

"What the fuck?" Sitka's voice came from behind me.

"A no would have been fine," I groaned.

"You stay the hell away from her. I saw the damage you did, you sick son of a bitch. Don't think for a minute that I would let you get anywhere near her." The young man growled. I snapped my eyes up to him immediately

"What are you talking about?" I asked. He held the picture back out to me.

"Her." I reached out and took the picture with my bloodied hand and turned it back around for him.

"This is my daughter, Isabel. She's missing." He looked at the picture again. I felt Ben's hand on my shoulder.

"He's telling the truth. I'm his brother, this is my niece we are searching for, she went missing three days ago." The kid sighed as though he was irritated.

"I am on my way to the hospital. I have to go."

"I just need to know if you have seen her, which by your reaction I would say you have." I could feel hope rising in my chest, she was alive, and she was here. I just needed to hear him say that it was her he had seen. I couldn't take another night lying in bed wondering where my child was.

"I have."

"Where is she?"

"I don't know." I could feel my stomach turning and I thought I was going to be sick. He was quiet for a minute. "I bet that I can find out, but I really have to get to the hospital."

"We will follow you there." Following this kid around wasn't part of my plans.

But he had seen my daughter.

As I climbed back into the truck, my thoughts became intrusive as I watched the young man disappear around the side of the building.

What if this was a trap?

When we arrived at the hospital, he got out of the car and quickly made his way inside.

"Does he?" Ben started.

"Yes. He does," I interrupted. I knew what he was asking. He looked remarkably like Jake. My mind played back to what he had said about the picture, calling Isabel, Katie. "Do you think it's her?" The question left my lips as I continued holding my arm over my nose.

"By the way he reacted, I would almost guarantee it."

"He's even protective of her like Jake," I sniffled. Memories of him began to run through my mind, of when he was a little boy in a car seat in the truck, to his graduation, to the day I reunited with him in the hospital after the girls were taken. His anger with me when I left, brought a heat to my chest.

I should have been there for them.

I shouldn't have taken off on another tour.

I was sad over losing Jen, the love of my life.

They were her gift to me.

Now, all I had left was Isabel, and I had to find her before I lost her to.

"Come on, let's get you checked out," Ben said. I nodded and we made our way inside.

Sitting in the waiting room, the young man from the bar was quietly talking to another gentleman. I checked in at the desk and then took a seat with Ben and the boys.

"Should have let me hit him," Sitka said quietly.

"Now, now, it was just a misunderstanding," Ben replied.

"Do you think he's working with Solomon?" Keone asked.

"I don't know," Ben replied. I heard a door creak open.

"Micheal Twain?" I stood and walked over to the door; I could feel the eyes of the young man from the bar as I walked by. I glanced at him briefly, noting the scar that ran over his eye into his cheek.

As I entered the door, the nurse took me back to triage and asked the big question.

"What happened?"

"I slipped and fell trying to walk out to my truck."

"Did you hit your head?"

"No, I stopped myself but bashed my nose off my arm." I wiggled my arm that had blood covering the sleeve.

"Okay, can you move your arm for me?" I pulled my arm away from my nose and she tipped my head back.

"I don't think you broke it; it's still bleeding a little bit. I'm going to have one of our doctors come in quick, we might be able to get you out of here without having to take you back, unless you want a full work up."

"The faster you can get me on my way the better." She nodded and walked away, leaving me alone in the room. The distant beeping sounds coming from the emergency treatment area, crept in under the door.

When she reappeared, she was followed by a man in a white jacket.

"Hi, Mr. Twain, I'm Dr. Azir, let me take a look at your really quick." I nodded and he pulled out a flashlight, putting it to my eyes. "Follow the light

please." I did as instructed. "Tip your head back."
I tipped my head back and he looked at my nose.
"Thank you." I put my head back down and he
put his flashlight back in his pocket.

"What's the verdict?"

"I'm going to send in a script for any pain that
might follow over the next few days. The bleeding
is mostly under control, but if it picks up again,
please come back and see me." He handed me a
few tissues, and I nodded my head.

"Thanks, doc." He nodded his head at me and
then at the nurse before he exited the room. I
stood up.

"Right this way, Mr. Twain," the nurse said quietly. I nodded and she led me back out into the
waiting room.

As I walked out into the waiting room, Ben,
Sitka, and Keone got to their feet.

"What did they say?" Ben asked.

"They just checked me over really quick and
told me I could go." Ben nodded. I looked over

where the young man had been sitting. He was no longer sitting there, but the man he had been sitting with, remained, holding his head in his hands. I knew that look all too well, a father who was concerned for the welfare of his child. I glanced up at the others quickly and then walked over and took the seat next to him.

"Are you alright?"

"No. I made a mistake."

"It can't be that bad."

"It's pretty bad." He sighed heavily and lifted his head, his eyes meeting mine. The tears in his eyes were evident. Before we could continue our conversation, the door opened, and the young man came back out.

"Sam?" the man said as he stood. I stood with him. Sam looked at the two of us as he walked closer. "How's Scarlett?" the man asked.

"She's going to be okay. I have to go."

"Where are you going?"

"The man that shot her." He stopped, his eyes meeting mine. A visible ache on his face at the words he was about to speak. "Took Isabel." His words hit me like bricks sending my heart into my stomach.

"Who did this?" the man asked. Sam dropped his gaze to the floor.

"Scarlett didn't say." The man dropped his gaze and Sam looked up at him. "She said you knew." The man lifted his head.

"A man would do anything to protect his children." There was something in Sam's reaction that brought anger to my chest, every word he spoke made me want to break the man's jaw. He had a hand in this, I could feel it coursing through my veins. I had to control myself; I didn't have time to deal with him.

"We can deal with that later, right now I have to find Isabel." The man nodded and then turned his attention to me.

"I'm so sorry."

"I'll deal with you later, after I get my daughter back. For your sake you better hope she is safe. So, help me if." I stopped. I couldn't bring myself to say the words the infiltrated my brain.

My voice was laced with anger, but more importantly it held a promise.

"I have to go," Sam said again.

"I'm coming with you," I said. Sam looked at me questioningly.

"She's my daughter." We stared at each other for a moment when the silence was broken by the sound of my phone. I pulled it from my pocket and Chuck's name flashed across the screen.

"One minute." Sam nodded and I answered the call.

"Chuck?"

"Mike, where are you?"

"Nashville. Isabel is here somewhere."

"Mike, we got something."

"What is it?" I looked at the faces of the men who stared back at me waiting for a response.

Chuck's words entered my ear, registering.

My body locked.

"Are you sure?" I asked. My ears ringing.

"Yes."

"Thank you." I hung up the phone and looked at them as their eyes were on me. Sam wanted to get going and Ben had questions in his eyes.

"What did he say?" Ben asked.

"They got something."

"What did they find?" Sitka asked. I looked at Sitka and then my eyes flicked from Sam as he was steps away on his phone to Ben.

"Weston Mills is alive, and he is here."

A shockwave coursed through the air as my words escaped into the open.

"How is this possible?"

"I don't know."

"Do they know where?" Ben asked.

"No." I stopped. "There's more." Ben looked at me with sharp curiosity.

My body shuddered as the words formed in my head.

"What is it?"

"Soren's body is missing."

CHAPTER 16

We went back to the bar, where Sam invited us upstairs to his apartment. He leaned against the counter, folding his arms across his chest.

"Where do we even start?" My eyes drifted to Keone as he stood in the small kitchen, the question hanging in the air.

"We have nothing to help us find Katie," Sam said.

"Isabel." I corrected him. Sam looked at me and nodded. There was a vibration in my pocket, and I reached, desperate to open the message that had come through.

"Got it," I said as the video played on the screen. Sam walked over and peered at the screen as I held it out for the others to see.

"What is it?"

"Camera footage of the street." I played it back for Sam and there was a black car. Isabel reached out to another woman. A man behind them raised his gun. As the shot fired, Sam turned away.

"How did you get that video?" he asked.

"I have connections."

"We should inform the police."

"No."

It flew from my mouth in desperation.

"They will kill her."

"They could go in quiet."

I got within an inch of our chests touching.

My shoulders square.

Jaw clenched.

He didn't understand.

"This isn't a game. This is my daughter's life."

He fell back a step, creating space.

While I remained, determined to make my point loud and clear.

"Then we should get going."

"I'm waiting to get more details about the car and where it went. There are cameras all over this city." I was hoping that with any luck Chuck and his crew would be able to find the car and give me an idea of where to go. The sooner we found these people and Isabel the better.

"You know a lot about Nashville." His statement caught me off guard.

"We used to live here. For Isabel's entire life until we moved about a year ago." He nodded and the room fell silent.

"What happened to your face?" I had noticed the scar on his face earlier and never asked. I needed something to distract me as I waited.

"I was in a motorcycle accident a little over eight months ago."

"Where are you from?"

"California."

"How did you end up in Nashville?" He seemed stunned by my question. Shaking his head he leaned against the counter again.

"I don't know how to explain it. I feel connected to it somehow and my Dad encouraged me to move; he set me up with a job at the bar and this apartment."

"Do you remember anything from your accident?"

"Not really."

I had him talking.

I had to know why he helped her.

"Why did you take my daughter in?"

"She found me when she made it into the bar Friday night. I tried to send her away, but she was terrified and had obviously been injured. I didn't have the heart to send her away, so I was still trying to figure out what happened before I involved anyone else."

"I can never thank you enough for all that you did for her." Our eyes locked and for a moment I saw Jake flash inside of him. He dropped his gaze. A flash of regret in his eyes made me instantly uneasy.

He was guilty.

But of what?

"We should start looking," he said. I nodded when my phone went off in my hand. I quickly opened the message as it had come from Chuck.

"They headed East, out of town." I started for the door as the others followed. It was halfway down the stairs that I realized Sam had gone back in.

As we piled into the truck, Sam approached handing me a piece of paper.

"This is my number in case you find something." I nodded, taking the paper, I quickly put the number in my phone and sent a call. His phone began ringing in his pocket.

"I'll be in touch." He nodded and then walked away. I looked down at the paper in my hand and saw creases from other writing. Turning it over, I saw scratching on the other side.

Scratches I recognized.

Freezing me in place.

"What is it?" Ben asked. I showed him the piece of paper.

"Isabel's handwriting." My hand trembled as I saw her delicate words on the paper. *"Your laugh, it reminds me of my brother."* My heart began to ache as I read the message over and over again.

He reminded her of Jake.

My poor, sweet girl, torn by the loss of her big brother.

It made my heart feel as though it was shredding in my chest.

"Do you want me to drive?" Ben asked, forcing me to break my eyes away from the paper. I sniffled and turned the paper back over.

"No, I got it."

"Are you sure?"

"Yes." I could see Sam pulling out of the alleyway and heading off down the road.

"There's something off about him."

"He seems like a good kid," Ben offered.

"I think he's hiding something."

"He reminds me of."

"Jake." I interrupted. Ben nodded and I could see him wince. He still blamed himself for what happened to my son, but there was nothing that boy wouldn't have done to save his sister. Even if Ben had been on the boat with them, Jake would still have given his life. I cleared my throat and put the truck in drive.

We spent most of the night cruising the East end. Sam, met up with us here and there to collectively discuss anything parties had found.

It was well after midnight when we headed back to Sam's and found his car parked out in front of the bar. He was leaning against the hood as we approached.

"Did you find anything?" I asked.

"No, you?"

"Nothing."

"It's like they completely disappeared." I put my hands on my head as my chest tightened.

"Have you tried to call your contact again, to see if they have any new information?" Sam asked.

"They are digging, but they aren't finding anything." I had been on and off with Chuck through most of the drive, but he always had the same answer, they were looking.

"Can't they track the car? It should have a GPS."

"It's disconnected."

"So, there's nothing left for us to do." It came out quietly and the realization hit me.

"Dammit!" I yelled as I kicked an empty beer can that had been abandoned on the sidewalk.

"Calm down, Mikey," Ben said as he grabbed my shoulders. I turned to him, anger rising from my chest.

"How can I? She is out there with God knows who and Solomon is going to walk free."

"Solomon?" Sam asked. I turned back to look at Sam.

"Do you know him?"

"No. But the name sounds familiar."

I looked at Ben. He nodded and I pulled my phone from my pocket. I walked away from the group and headed toward the truck.

"Mike?" Chuck answered, his voice weary.

"Chuck, can you look into a Samuel Milier for me, out of San Francisco?"

"Why?"

"Because my daughter was staying with him. I need to know everything you can tell me about this kid."

"Do you think he is involved?"

He seemed to care about her.

That's what made it harder to decide where trust lied.

"I don't know. The last thing I want to do is waste any more time on a wild goose chase with this kid, if he is."

"Understood. I've got it written down. Stay close to your phone, I'll be calling."

"Thanks Chuck."

"Be safe, Mike."

"Will do." I ended the call and went back to the group. As much as I hated to do it, I knew that there was nothing that could be done this late at night.

"Load up guys, we are going back to the house."

"What about Isabel?" Keone asked.

"There's nothing we can do tonight."

She was gone.

Again.

No leads.

Nothing.

Just…

Gone.

The words left a bad taste in my mouth.

I wanted to find my daughter and take her back home where she would be safe.

Soren was dead.

Now Solomon would walk free.

Even if she came running into my arms, where I so desperately wanted her. We would never make it back in time.

There was no stopping it.

Solomon Cross would be free.

My stomach turned inside out, and I rushed over to the truck and began to revolt by the tailgate.

"Mike?" Ben called. I held my hand out.

"I'm okay," I said as I spit out the vile taste in my mouth.

"What is it?"

"Nothing, just give me a minute."

After taking a few minutes to gather myself, I walked back over.

"Let's go." I looked at Sam. "We will be back in a little bit."

"I'll call you if I hear anything," he said. I nodded and we got into the truck. As we left, Sam walked down the alleyway, disappearing into the night.

CHAPTER 17

I was sitting on the back porch with a brandy in my hand. The cold bit at me profusely, but I didn't mind it, it reminded me that I was here, that I existed at all, despite the feeling of fading away. The night was quiet as snow gracefully fell from the dark sky. I sipped the warming liquid, staring out into the backyard. Memories began dancing in my mind's eye, of my kids, playing in the snow back here when they were little, building snowmen and having snowball fights.

Their sweet innocent laughter filled the hollow space.

Then it vanished, like a breath.

The silence was broken by the ringing of my cell phone. I pulled it from the table and saw Chuck's name appear on the screen. I pounded the button with my thumb and held the phone to my ear.

"Chuck?"

"Mike, I looked into the kid."

"What did you find?"

"I scoured everything that was sent to me from San Francisco, and everything checks out."

"What does?" I put the glass of brandy down on the table and rose to my feet.

"Samuel Milier was born in San Francisco, to William and Tana Milier. There are birth certificates, property documents, accident records, marriage licenses, school records, contracts. They sent me everything they could on this kid and his family. I even have his blood type." I felt my chest tighten at his words.

"Anything else?"

"A death certificate and an obituary."

"For whom?"

"Shaelyn Milier."

"Who is she?"

"Samuel's sister who passed away at the age of ten, from brain cancer." My heart fell into my stomach.

"How long ago was that?"

"From the dates, it looks like about seven years ago." I shook my head and dropped my gaze to my boots. That would explain why he felt the need to help Isabel, he was an older brother once too and still had that instinct. I cleared my throat, pushing back thoughts of Jake as they began to surface and got back to the task at hand.

"Do you think he is working for Solomon?"

"I don't know. He doesn't have a criminal record."

"What about the parents?"

"They're clean." I rubbed my face with my hand and sighed heavily. "Mike, what are you going to do?"

"I'm going to get this figured out. I have to do whatever it takes to find my daughter."

"Don't do anything stupid, Mike," Chuck said. I felt a smile crease into the corners of my lips.

"Whatever it takes." I hung up the phone. Putting it back in my pocket I turned and picked up the glass of brandy and threw it back.

I walked into the house and found Ben sitting at the table.

"Get your coat," I said as I walked through, grabbing my keys from the counter.

"Where are we going?" he asked.

"We are going back to Sam's."

"Did he hear something?" Ben asked as he stood, pulling his coat from behind the chair and slinging it over his shoulders.

"No."

"Then why are we going over there?" I turned and looked at him.

"I just want to keep looking and I'm willing to bet he's up still." Ben cocked a curious eyebrow at me.

"Do you think he is working with Solomon?"

"Chuck says he's clean."

"Then what's wrong?"

"He's too clean."

"What do you mean?"

"I don't know, but that's why I want to go over. I want to see if he knows something about where Isabel is and is keeping it from me."

"Do you want me to get the boys?"

"No. Make sure your loaded, because I'm going to do whatever it takes to bring my baby home." Ben nodded and he reached for his waist, pulling his pistol free. Dropping the magazine, he nodded with approval as he inspected it quickly. Slamming it back into place with a click he put it back and we headed to the door.

As we pulled up to the curb, outside of Sam's apartment, my heart dropped. His car that he had left parked on the street was now gone.

My stomach began doing backflips.

Had he lied to us?

Was he working with Solomon and snuck back out to wherever Isabel was after we left?

I threw the truck in park and pulled my phone free from my pocket. I quickly hit the call button under Sam's contact.

"Hey, you've reached Sam. I can't come to the phone right now." I hung up and dialed again. Once more it went straight to voicemail. I felt my breaths becoming ragged as I called it once more, only to receive the same message yet again. I slammed my phone down on the center console.

"What is it?" Ben asked.

"He's not answering. It's going straight to voicemail."

"This isn't looking good Mikey." I nodded. Picking up my phone again, I screenshot the contact for Sam and sent it to Chuck.

Within a few short minutes my phone began buzzing in my hand.

"Chuck."

"What do you need me to do?" His voice appeared more alert, instead of groggy as I had woken him earlier.

"I need a track on that phone. Sam's gone and I'm willing to bet wherever he is, Isabel is there."

"I'm running it now." I looked over at Ben as he lit a cigarette and his eyes met mine, as we waited in the silence.

It seemed like forever before Chuck returned.

"I have it."

"Where is it?"

"It's pinging from a tower about ten miles southwest of you."

"What's around there?"

"Looks like a giant forest, maybe a park."

"Percy Warner. Send me the exact coordinates, that place is too large to cover with just a location."

"I'll send them over right now." Within seconds the phone pinged in my ear, and I pulled it away, looking at what Chuck had sent me. I quickly put the phone back against my head, holding it with my shoulder as I slammed the truck into drive.

"Thanks, Chuck."

"Mike, you should get back up to cover you."

"I'll call them when I get there. I don't want to spook him. If he has Isabel and is working with Solomon, we both know she would be dead before they got there."

"Just be careful."

"Will do." I ended the call and tossed my phone to Ben.

"Pull those up." I hit the gas, pulling away from the curb into the street. "We are going to get my daughter back."

Driving as the GPS instructed me, my heart thundered.

I would break every law to reach Isabel in time.

When we pulled into a parking lot, I immediately recognized Sam's car. We got out, closing the doors quietly. Grabbing a flashlight, I put it in my back pocket. Ben's pistol clicked as he switched off the safety. I didn't know what we would find, but if anything, I was hoping we would find Isabel. Motioning with my hand, we began to walk towards the head of the trail.

We came across a car, abandoned on the pathway.

It was the black car.

The license plate a match.

About thirty feet away from the car, I could hear voices trailing up to us from off the path. They were distant. I stood quietly, begging my heart to settle so that I could make out the words that were coming from them. Hoping to hear anything that might relate to Isabel. There was grunting almost like one would hear if they were watching a fight.

"That's enough!" I heard it clear as day, and my eyes locked with Ben's. Whether my daughter was here or not, that voice came from someone that wasn't Sam. He wasn't alone. We began to stealthily make our way towards the voices, careful not to alert them to our presence.

As we got closer, the voices became clearer. My heart fell in my chest and I picked up the pace, when I heard a voice that I recognized cry out.

PART THREE

Sam

CHAPTER 18

I felt arms snake around me, hugging me tightly from behind, a head pressed to my back.

She was back.

Looking down, I was startled when I didn't see the well-manicured hands that I was accustomed to but instead bruised and blood-stained knuckles. My heart raced as I spun around unsure of what I would find. I forced the arms off me and grabbed the shoulders of a girl I didn't recognize.

She was filthy.

Crushed leaves tangled in her hair.

Tears streaking through the grime on her face.

Her striking blue eyes wide.

Fear-ridden.

There was a flash in my mind as her eyes met mine and I squeezed my eyes shut before shaking my head clear of the irritation, returning my attention to her. I felt my eyes harden as they landed on her once more.

"How the hell did you get in here?" Her face contorted into a sob and tears continued to run down her face. I looked around the room, looking for Rolf, the other bouncer. I felt a hand on my shoulder.

"Sam?" Jared asked. I blocked him out and turned my attention back to the girl.

"Who let you in here?" I stopped when my eyes caught the blood on her hands. "Jesus... kid, what happened to you?" Her eyes softened and a tear slipped down her cheek. She didn't respond and I felt uneasy, taking a good look at her. This girl had been through the ringer. I looked around again for someone that might be looking for her. Finally, spotting Rolf at the door, he seemed completely unaware that she was even here as he continued to focus on the door crowd.

"Sam, who the fuck is this?" Jared asked as he towered over her.

"I don't know." She shrunk away from him as he stood with his arms crossed over his chest, crowding her.

"Well, she can't be here, get rid of her before Alec sees her." I nodded, he was right, if my boss caught this girl in here, I could lose my job. I spun her around and with my hands on her shoulders moving her back through the crowd, towards the back door. Opening it, I walked her outside, the frigid air smacking us both with its bite. She spun on me then, loosening the grip I held on her shoulders. I was met by terrified eyes, before they darted around the empty alleyway.

"Go home." I pointed off into the night and turned to head back inside when I felt her grab my arm shakily and I spun back around.

"What do you want?" It came out harshly; it had been a long night and I was tired. I didn't have time to deal with this too.

She straightened, her head held high.

My breath caught when I saw her neck.

Deep bruises.

Finger-shaped.

Fresh and angry.

Something ugly tightened in my chest.

She sighed and my eyes found hers again before she stepped away.

The defeat in them sawing at me.

I felt the tension in my face dissipate as she pressed her back against the brick wall and slid down. Wrapping her arms around her legs, her chin resting on her knees.

She trembled.

I sighed.

Shaking my head.

I couldn't leave her like this.

"Are you okay?" I asked. My voice softened.

She didn't need shit from a bouncer.

She needed help.

She shook her head. I closed the door to the bar to silence the music as it spilled out. Where she sat, the light from the nearby streetlight cast a luminance around her. My heart thundered as I took in her pitiful appearance.

She couldn't have been older than sixteen.

Maybe younger.

I looked at my watch; it was well past curfew.

"Sam!" I turned around and saw Jared, standing at the end of the alleyway. "Come on man, it's busy as hell."

"Give me a minute." I looked at her again. The bars will be emptying soon.

If I left her, she could get hurt and I would spend my nights wondering if I made the right decision.

If I took her in, I could be incriminated or worse.

A double-edged sword.

I sighed.

"Come with me." I held out my hand to her, and she took it gently. Slowly, I pulled her to her feet and led her deeper into the alley. Pulling the next door in the alley open, I led her up the stairs.

Pushing into the apartment, I rushed her inside. Holding her at arms-length, in the well-lit area of the entryway, I could see the marks more clearly. She trembled under my hands and tears spilled silently down her face.

This girl wasn't running from something; she was running from someone.

What the hell was I doing?

"Is someone after you?" I asked. She silently stared at me, her head gently nodding. I instantly felt pity building in my heart as I took in her sorry disposition. My eyes wandered over to the clock on the wall, it was already after one in the morning, and the bar would be shutting down soon, which meant I had to get back to work, but what was I going to do with this girl? I looked back at her, her eyes still trained on me, pleading for help.

"I have to go back downstairs and close down the bar." I looked down the hall. "You can clean up and wait here for me until I get back, but then you are going to tell me what the hell is going on. I want to help you, but I don't have time right this second." She nodded and her gaze went to the floor.

"Come on." I walked by her and quickly led her to the bathroom. Disappearing into the room across the hallway, I quickly returned with a t-shirt and sweatpants. She was still standing there, quietly. I handed her the clothes.

"I'll be back in about two hours." She nodded and gently took the clothes from me. She entered the bathroom, and I walked back down the hall toward the steps, heading back to the bar. Closing the door behind me, the strangest thing happened. I stuck my key in the door and locked it before walking away. Pulling the key from the door, the moment struck me as unusual, I normally never locked the top door. The thumping of the music downstairs broke me from my thoughts, and I quickly made my way back down.

I hated leaving her alone... but I didn't see another choice.

When I entered the bar, Jared was leaning against the counter.

"Who the hell was that?" Jared asked.

"I have no idea."

"How did she get in?"

"I don't know, I didn't see her come through the front."

"That damn barback must have left the back door unlocked again."

"Maybe."

"Did you send her back to wherever she came from." I cleared my throat at his question.

"I couldn't take her to the cops looking like that. Not without answers first." I crossed my arms across my chest as I awaited the inevitable tirade.

"Are you crazy? Some minor girl comes in off the street, and you take her to your apartment and leave her alone?"

"What was I supposed to do? I had to get back in here. Also, it's freezing out there and she clearly had nowhere to go."

"So, you just adopting random kids off the street now?""Don't start with me."

"You should call the police."

"I don't know man, something isn't right with her."

"What do you mean? Like she's crazy or something?"

"No. She had bruises on her neck, and her face. She seemed downright terrified. I think she might be in danger."

"She told you that?" I thought back to our small moment in the hallway. How she didn't speak a word to me.

"Not in so many words."

"That's fucked up." I nodded my head in agreement. "Did she at least tell you her name?"

"No. I told her she could clean up and that we would talk after the shift. She seemed to understand."

"Do you want me to close up by myself, so you can go take care of that?"

"No. Alec will kill me if I miss another closing."

"What about Scarlett?" My mind floated to the beautiful woman that I was lucky enough to call mine. She was Alec's daughter, and this very bar was named after her. She was one of the kindest and sweetest people I had ever met. She was on vacation with her college friends in Panama, I'm sure she would understand, but if I could figure this out without involving her, then I would.

"She isn't due back for three more days. I'm sure I can get this thing figured out before then." Jared nodded and then there came the obvious sound of glass shattering. Looking across the bar, a fight began to break out. Voices rose in the back of the bar and then a chair crashed against the wall, followed by more breaking glass.

"Showtime."

As I moved toward the fight, the noise of the bar swallowed everything.

Her face appeared in the blur.

The bruises on her neck.

Suddenly I knew.I had just stepped into something that wouldn't let me go.

CHAPTER 19

B y the time I got back to my apartment it was quarter after three. I had tissues stuffed in one nostril as I had taken a swing to the face.

The consequence of trying to break up the fight. I was certain I would have a black eye in the morning. Stretching my face, trying to ease the soreness that resided. I reached for the door, turning the knob only for it to stop, reminding me that I had locked it when I left.

I had no idea what I was walking into, there was a good chance this girl robbed me blind and was already gone.

I half-expected to walk into a trashed apartment.

Inhaling and exhaling deeply, I put the key in the knob and unlocked the door.

As the door slowly creaked open, the hallway was clear, the light was on as I usually left it. I stepped in, quietly closing the door behind me as I began to make my way through. The first place I went to was the bathroom.

The door was shut, and I knocked but received no response.

I gently pushed it open, the familiar smell of Scarlett's shampoo and body scrub, washed over me as I entered.

Damp towel on the hook.

Dirty clothes on the floor.

Muddy shoes stacked by the clothes.

I picked up a hoodie, a shirt falling out from within.

Pulling the shirt free, I held it in my hand.

Dark burgundy smudges.

My eyes widening.

Blood.

In several different places.

I stared at it, wondering if they belonged to her or someone else.

Her face appeared.

Her bloodied knuckles.

It had to be hers.

Shaking my head, I walked out of the bathroom, closing the door behind me. Crossing the hallway, I entered my bedroom, where I threw the clothes into the dirty hamper. I looked at them as they rested on the top and couldn't help but wonder what had happened.

She didn't seem dangerous but she sure as hell was scared.

Exiting the room, I quietly walked down the hallway. At the end I turned my head to the right to look into the living room.

The kitchen light over the sink was on, illuminating the back of the couch. Cautiously, I got closer and peered over the edge. To my surprise the girl was curled into a ball, sleeping. I felt a chill run down my spine as the cold snap in the apartment touched me.

If I was cold then she had to be freezing.

Walking back out into the hallway, I opened the closet to find a blanket. The first one I grabbed was a thick one that my Dad had sent with me when I moved to Nashville. Taking it, I wandered back into the living room, slowly draping it over the mysterious girl on my couch. A yawn escaped me. Whatever was going on could wait until tomorrow, I didn't have the energy to have a lengthy conversation nor the heart to wake her up.

Heading back across the hall to the kitchen, I turned out the light.

In my bedroom, I threw on my pajama bottoms and tossed my black t-shirt into the overflowing laundry basket. I walked into the bathroom, pulling the tissue from my nostril. I tossed it into the trash and looked into the mirror, staring at the faded scar that trailed from above my eyebrow, across my eye and into my cheek as it mocked me. Despite having thirty stitches in my face, it looked better than it had.

Flashes began to take over behind my eyes, sending my head into a chaotic fit of pain. I put my hands on either side of the sink, gripping it until my knuckles were white and took heavy breaths, trying to make it go away.

As it began to cease, I opened my eyes and in that moment the blue eyes of the sleeping girl on my couch flashed.

The fear behind them was nothing short of evident.

I shook my thoughts away as another yawn escaped me, walking out and heading across the hall to my bedroom.

Crawling into bed, I turned the light out and folded my hands behind my head, staring at the ceiling. Sleep was gnawing at me, but so were questions about this girl.

Where the hell did she come from?

Why did she approach me at the bar?

Who did that to her?

As the question crept into my mind, I felt a sense of anger rising.

Whoever did that to her must be some kind of monster.

The bruises on her neck flashed into my mind.

Whoever she is running from was angry, the depth of the marks on her neck, enough to...

I stopped myself; a shudder ran through my body thinking about how anyone could do that to a child.

I rolled over and tried to push the girl from my mind, so I could sleep.

Even as sleep took hold, she lingered.

It was the sound of a knock on the door that pulled me from sleep.

I got up groggily and opened the door.

The girl stood, staring down the hallway in front of my door.

I stepped out.

A dark figure loomed at the door.

How did they get in?

I know I had locked it.

"Who are you? What are you doing here?" The figure cocked its head toward me quickly before shifting their direction back to her.

I looked at her.

A pulse made her shift unnaturally.

Her eyes widened and I heard the thundering steps quicken.

I stepped out, colliding with the figure. Locked in an immediate fight.

For her.

"Run!" I gave what I had, but they were stronger, pushing me away. My back slamming against the wall.

I watched helplessly as she stood, frozen in fear.

Tears in her eyes.

Grabbing her by the arm, they spun. Tears glistened on her face in the dim glow from the stairwell light.

Her fearful eyes scanned my face with a silent plea.

Her chest heaving.

A knife appeared at her throat.

Something inside of me broke as anger rose in my chest.

"Let her go!" The words echoed.

I scrambled to my feet to get to them when her head ripped back.

The knife sharper.

A whimper escaping as a dark line began to slip down her neck.

"Look man, I don't know what she did, but this...this is crazy."

The figure didn't move, just stood there, staring at me in the dark.

At least, that's how it felt.

Moonlight reconfigured and under the darkness, I could see just a little of his face.

Familiar.

Yet unidentifiable.

Tension gripped my chest.

Long fingers of fate, squeezing my heart.

Unrelenting.

I had to save her.

"She's just a kid."

My eyes flicked to her.

Her hands were wrapped around his forearm.

Tears still falling.

Trembling.

The room tilted with a flash, from hallway to entryway.

A door.

Stairs.

Gone.

I looked at him again.

The hallway returned.

"Let her go, and we can pretend it never happened."

In the glow, I saw him smirk.

Ripping the blade.

The sound of steel cutting through flesh.

My heart stopped.

Screams filled the air.

My own.

Someone else's.

I wasn't sure.

I shot straight up, forcing back the weight of the blankets.

The sound of a car rattling down the street grounding me.

Then a scream resounding into the physical world from my internal chaos.

I ran out into the hallway; the screaming echoed until there was nothing left.

Silence quickly became the only thing drafting through the hall. My chest heaving as I leaned against the wall, trying to piece together what the hell that nightmare was about and what it meant.

Who had been here and why were they after her?

Rubbing my eyes, I walked towards the living room.

As I neared, the sound of desperate gasps, launched me to her side.

My eyes found her in the dark.

I froze.

She was writhing.

Chest lifted.

Head pinned back.

It was when she suddenly stopped moving and I couldn't hear her breathing anymore that my feet moved forward taking her by the shoulders. She sat up almost instantly, her blue eyes piercing mine as they were filled with panic and dried tears stained her cheeks. She began to breathe heavily again, but it quickly turned to choking. Her head fell back, her blonde hair draping over my arms.

"How do I help?" I asked, panic rising in my chest. I didn't know this girl, but I couldn't let her die in my apartment, I would be implicated, and I still didn't know anything about her.

She reached for her throat.

Her hand fell weakly back into her lap.

Immediately I recognized the signs; it was a panic attack.

I gently rested her back down on the couch.

Rushing to the kitchen, I threw open a drawer and found an old inhaler from a few months ago.

It rattled when I shook it.

Still had something left.

Taking it back to her, I knelt down, handing it to her, she raised her hand, and it fell again. I pulled the cap off and put it in her mouth, hitting the plunger. Another bright flash danced behind my eyes.

Sirens blaring in my ears.

I shook my head; I had to focus to help her right now. As I pulled the little plastic tube from her mouth her breathing settled, and she exhaled heavily, as she seemed to relax from the medicine entering her lungs. I put the cap back on and put it on the coffee table.

"I'm going to leave this here; you can have it."

I heard the concern in my own voice as I shook.

I too had been a victim to many sleepless nights.

My own demons.

My mind raced back to that day. I didn't remember much, just what my parents had told me. I had gone out riding with my friends on our motorcycles; a car had run a red light and hit me as I went through. A storm had begun, and we were trying to get back to the house. I ended up going over the hood and into the windshield.

Vaguely, I remembered the thunder and lightning, and being hit by rain, but nothing else. It was all a giant blur. I could feel the tension rising in my chest as my mind raced through the past months since then, trying to make sense of it all.

A hand on my arm broke me from my thoughts, she was sitting up, and her blue eyes were looking into mine, illuminated by the light from the kitchen.

Getting to my feet I rubbed the back of my head. Her sleepiness was evident as she swayed back and forth slightly.

"Go back to sleep and we will talk in the morning." She nodded and laid back, curling up into a ball on the couch. After placing the blanket over her, I padded across the room and took a seat in the chair. In the light I could see her watching me from the couch. I had so many things I wanted to ask her, but right now she needed to sleep. I wasn't going to induce another attack by hurling a barrage of questions. She seemed comfortable, which was a good start.

I still felt a rush of uneasiness inside, but I wasn't sure if it was her presence or knowing that there was likely someone out there, looking for this girl.

With what intentions, who could say.

But the damage done to her led me to believe that they were evil.

She shifted on the couch, closing her eyes.

I sat there until I heard her gently breathing. She had fallen back asleep and from what I could tell, she was peaceful. Part of me questioned if I should stay out here and keep an eye on her in case she needed anything.

Here I was a man, twenty-two years old, bringing in a stray teenage girl from the streets. The thought was crazy in my head, but she as far as I knew was alone and from what I could see, she needed help. I quietly yawned and let my head fall back against the chair. If it wasn't for the stiffness I felt in my body from the fight, then I would stay right here. Getting up slowly so as not to wake her, I tiptoed out of the room and back down the hall to my bedroom.

Lying in bed, my mind was racing, the nightmare, the girl, her panic attack. She was clearly afraid, but not of me. Part of me wanted to go back out there and ask her some questions, looking at the clock, it was five in the morning. They would have to wait for a little bit longer. I settled back into bed, the quietness, settling my mind enough for me to fall into slumber.

Her eyes flashed through my mind.

Bruises.

The sound of glass breaking.

Disembodied screams.

Thunder booming in the distance.

Everything became muffled.

Like I was underwater.

I shot up and looked at the clock; I had only dozed off for about thirty minutes. Screeching tires pierced my ears. I covered them, trying to silence it. Breathing heavily, I flopped back against my pillows. My brain was in a fight with the few memories I had and this girl. Mixing the two together, causing my head to throb. I ran my hands down my face, despite the soreness that resided, trying to remember more about that day. Wondering why my brain was playing this horrid game of mashup.

I wasn't unaccustomed to late nights with the echoes of my past.

Now this girl was here.

Out of thin air.

No idea who she was.

Where she came from.

Why she was running.

Who she was running from.

The thought of her shifted something deep.

Internal.

Her presence was affecting me, melting together with things I was trying to forget.

CHAPTER
20

When I woke up again, my head was throbbing. Memory fogged from the fight at the bar. The guy's fist catching my nose.

It still ached.

There was something else.

My heart froze.

The girl.

Her eyes.

The marks.

I stumbled out of bed, ripping the door open, spilling into the hallway.

A quiet shuffling came from down the hall.

Metal catching off metal.

With quick but quiet steps, I made my way towards the noise.

Entering the kitchen, she was at the stove, eggs sizzling in a pan.

My gaze shifted to the table. Where orange juice and toast had been placed.

I could smell the raisin toast in the air.

It had been a while since I had breakfast that wasn't from a takeout container.

"What are you doing?"

Startled, she jerked in my direction.

I walked towards her.

Her shoulders tensed and I stopped.

"Not much of a talker are you?"

I could physically see her shoulders relax.

She shrugged, turning her attention back to the stove.

I felt a pang of guilt in my chest. I approached slowly and stood next to her. Her eyes cast sideways at me for a moment before she turned her eyes back to the pan.

"I need to ask you some questions." She gently shook her head.

"Are you in danger?"

She hesitated.

A lump clawed its way into my throat.

Then came the nod, I feared.

"Why don't you talk?" She stopped pushing the eggs around in the pan and let go of the spatula. Holding her hand out palm upwards, she used her other hand to signal writing.

"Pen and paper?" She nodded. I opened the junk drawer a few drawers down and pulled out a pen and paper. I tossed them down on the counter beside her.

Her body shifted at the sound.

I recognized it right away, guilt pooling in my chest.

A trauma response.

Her eyes met mine.

She looked at the paper and pen on the counter.

Raising an eyebrow, she looked at me and nodded her head towards the stove.

"Right. It can wait. But I need to know everything." She kept her eyes on the stove. "I'm sticking my neck out here for you kid. I deserve to know why."

She nodded softly.

Picking up the pen and paper, I went to the table and sat down. Softly, I placed the paper and pen on the table.

Grabbing the paper, I let the noise of the world distract me.

A plate clinked off the table.

Folding the paper and putting it down, she took a seat across from me.

It was odd.

She was comfortable.

She went through my kitchen, finding everything she needed to make breakfast.

I wasn't sure if I found it intrusive or unexpectedly kind.

I picked up my fork.

She picked up the pen.

"Who are you?" I asked as I took a bite of the eggs. They were fluffy and well-seasoned, reminding me of a time when I was younger. The pen made scratching noises as she wrote.

"Who are you?"

"I asked you first." She cocked her head at me. Of course, she wasn't going to tell me anything without a little bit of trust, she was on the run. "My name is Sam Milier." Dropping her gaze, she set the pen down and dashed away a silent tear before lifting her juice.

"Where did you come from?" She shook her head, like she didn't want to tell me.

"We agreed you would tell me everything." She sighed and jotted something down.

"Here."

"Why were you in the bar last night and why did you come up to me?" I watched as she squinted her eyes slightly, as though she was forcing back tears, before she began to scratch on the pad of paper once again.

"You look familiar."

"How so? How old are you?" The questions flew out of my mouth.

Faded ghosts rose from the grave.

Glass shattered.

Thunder followed.

I felt the anxiety in my chest but ignored it.

My jaw tightened.

I had to focus.

I heard the scratching on the paper stop.

"You remind me of someone from my past. I'm sixteen." She put the pen down and picked up her fork, pushing the eggs around on her plate before taking a miniscule bite. Putting the fork down she picked up her orange juice and took a small sip.

As I watched her, I felt a strange sense of calm. My headache began to subside, and I internally scolded my subconscious. I had never seen the reports of the accident, I only knew what my parents had told me. Everything had been handled before I was even out of the hospital, and they told me not to worry about it. I watched her pushing the eggs around again, she seemed unsure of what to do as we sat in the uncomfortable silence.

Her eggs going cold.

Her toast buttered, untouched.

Her fingerprints caught in the sunlight on the glass.

Evidence she was here.

That could be a problem later.

I shoved the thought away immediately.

Focusing back on her lack of appetite.

"Aren't you hungry?" I asked.

She shrugged her shoulders.

Her color pale.

Her eyes lethargic.

She needed to eat something.

The memory of her, that first moment, she had been in the elements for sure, for how long it was hard to tell. I shook the thoughts away and asked the question I needed the answer to the most.

"Who are you?" Her entire demeanor changed as though she had become frozen.

Only for a moment.

She picked up the pen again.

The instant the pen scratched against the paper's grain, a soft click came from down the hallway.

One I recognized.

The front door.

Closing.

CHAPTER 21

B efore I could get my ass out of my seat, she blew in like a summer breeze. Her gentle deep, brown hair cascading unbothered down her back, her skin kissed by the Panama sun, the smell of her perfume, intoxicating. Her bright topaz eyes were wide with happiness, until they landed on the girl sitting at the table. My eyes locked on her, her beauty taking the air from my lungs.

"Babe, you're back early," I forced out.

"Who the hell is this?" Her voice shook with the question as she stared wide eyed at the girl sitting at the table, wearing one of my t-shirts and sweatpants. I stood, taking a place next to her as I looked back at the girl. Her head down and I could see her shoulders tremble.

"Come with me to the bedroom." I put my arm around Scarlett's waist and led her down the hall-way.

"Sam, who the hell is that?" she asked as I closed the door. Her voice was shaking now.

"I'm still trying to figure that out."

"Where did she come from?"

"She showed up at the bar last night."

"Sam, that's an underage girl. Did you tell my Dad?" I rubbed the back of my neck.

"Not, exactly."

"Why not?"

"She was terrified, babe. All I could think to do was get her out of there."

"By bringing her here?"

"Something happened to her."

"What do you mean?"

"Did you get a good look at her?"

"Not really."

"Her throat is bruised, like someone tried to choke her to death." Scarlett took my hands in hers, pulling me to sit down on the bed with her. I could feel my heart pounding, as I exhaled heavily, realizing that my pulse was racing.

"You should call the police." I shook my head.

"Something doesn't seem right about it."

"What do you mean?"

"I don't know. I wanted to ask her before I did that. What if the person who hurt her is someone she lives with? They could kill her next time."

"Babe, she should be with people who can help her. What can you do for her?" My eyes fell to the floor as I searched for answers.

She was right.

What was I going to do?

How could I help her?

"She's not our problem." My eyes snapped up to her. "You're right. She's not our problem. She's my problem."

Scarlett sighed heavily.

"That came out wrong. What I'm trying to say is this isn't up for you to handle."

"I have to help her, babe. I don't know why, I can't explain it, but I felt compelled to. Last night the bar was busy as hell and out of everyone, she came to me." She stood and her hands found their way onto my shoulders.

"Do you think maybe she felt safe with you?"

"I don't know." She gripped my upper arms. Squeezing my biceps with quiet warning.

"Well, you better figure it out and soon. My Dad won't hesitate to call the cops if he catches her in the bar."

"I don't plan on taking her down there."

"If she ran in once and found you, she might do it again." I nodded, that was definitely a risk.

"I'll talk to her."

"I'm going to be at home, if you need any-thing."

"Do you have some clothes that you are willing to part with? I gave her a t-shirt and sweats, but I don't have anything else that would fit her."

"Didn't she come with clothes?"

"She's not a doll babe." She tilted her head at me, glaring at me underneath her eyelashes. "Just the ones she was wearing, and they are filthy, I need to wash them."

"I'll go home and check. I'm sure I have some-thing. How old is she?"

"Sixteen."

"Alright, well I'll come back in a little bit, maybe Taylor has some old clothes, they might be about the same size." I nodded and she planted a soft kiss on my cheek. Pulling away her eyes met mine. "Be careful, Sam." Before, I could respond she had opened the door and sashayed out into the hallway. By the time I hit the hallway, I heard the click of the lock engage as she disappeared from the apartment. I ran my fingers through my hair and headed back into the kitchen.

Entering the food was still on the table, but the girl was gone. I looked at the paper and saw that she had begun to write something.

"Hello?" I called. Feeling like an idiot I huffed. She wasn't going to respond. I approached the couch and to my surprise, there she was, curled up, sleeping. I really wanted to know who she was and how she came to be here. A chill drafted through the room, and I felt a shiver rattle me. Grabbing the blanket, I covered her and went back into the kitchen.

I tidied up the leftovers. Her plate was barely touched. I wrapped it and shoved it in the fridge, suddenly aware she couldn't live on eggs, butter, beer, and milk. Closing the door, I returned to collecting the dishes. Wiping the table, I picked up the pen and paper. Looking at it, her responses stopped me.

"You look familiar." I read it over and over again.

Grasping for a connection.

A memory.

Something to make the fractures heal.

But nothing came.

Maybe I looked like someone she knew.

Maybe that's why she approached me at the bar.

There was still so much I didn't know.

I heard shuffling in the other room and wandered off to check on her in case she was having another panic attack. A weird relief filled me when I saw she was fine and just getting up. Looking at the clock she had been napping a little over an hour. She groggily sat up and looked at me. I leaned against the archway and crossed my arms over my chest.

"We really need to have this talk." She nodded and held out her hand, for the paper and pen. Grabbing them from the kitchen table, I walked around the couch, handing them to her before taking a seat on the other end.

"Start with your name." The pen scratched the paper.

She turned it toward me. The name scribbled over something she had begun to write earlier. Letters that looked different from the one that appeared. S-a, covered by darker ink.

"Katie?" I read it out loud. She nodded.

I pushed away the odd way it was written.

"What happened to you Katie?" Sliding it back, she scratched again and then hesitated as she shakily showed it to me.

"Lost my voice." She gently touched the dip just at the base of her throat and sadness filled her eyes as she shook her head.

"How?" She picked up the pen.

Hesitating.

An obvious tremble in her hand as she scratched the paper again.

"Attacked."

"They took your voice?" She nodded again and I watched a single tear slide down her cheek.

"Who did this to you?" More scratching.

"Someone dangerous."

My heart skipped a beat. I looked at her, cocking an eyebrow.

"I'm going to need more than that."

She put the pen down and pulled her legs to her chest.

"Is it someone you live with?" Your parents? A sister? A brother?" Her teary eyes met mine when the word brother entered the air.

Choking me.

I had a sister once, but she had died young. My memory of her was nonexistent after the accident, but my parents reminded me.

I could never have done that to her.

Could her brother have done this?

The thought made my heart ache.

"Did your brother do this to you?" She ferociously shook her head and picked up the pen again. As she finished scribbling she turned it around.

"A stranger."

My heart sank.

"Why would a stranger attack you?" She dropped her head. More questions came to mind, but I couldn't bring myself to ask them, seeing she had become upset.

How could anyone do this?

Why?

Why her?

I would have to circle back to those questions later, deciding to change the subject to learn more.

"How did you end up in the bar."

"The back door was unlocked." She wrote. I chuckled a little bit.

"Well, it's not supposed to be." A small smile appeared in the corners of her mouth.

"Parents?" She wrote one word.

"Dead."

"Your brother?" She nodded at the paper. I pointed at the last word she wrote. The question in my eyes.

Unspoken.

With a tear slipping down her cheek, she nodded.

My chest collapsed, air thickening in my lungs.

She had lost everyone.

We sat in silence briefly.

"Why did you approach me?" Her eyes flicked to me for a moment.

She scratched again.

Her response was simple.

"Your laugh. It reminds me of my brother."

All the answers I anticipated vanished.

"I sound like your brother," I sighed. She was resting her head on her arms; her face dampened as tears billowed from her eyes.

She opened her mouth, and nothing came out but a strangled cry.

Her face was the silent picture of immeasurable grief.

My heart began to ache.

She was attacked.

Her voice stolen.

She had lost everyone she loved.

She put her hand over her mouth, her eyes squeezed shut as though she were willing the tears and heartache to stop. I moved closer to her and her eyes opened. They were red from crying, making her irises pop in color. Before I could offer any sort of comforting words, she fell against me, resting her head on my arm. I could feel her shaking as she leaned against me. I remained stunned for a moment, before relenting and wrapping my arm around her shoulders, gently hugging her.

For no reason at all, I rested my head against hers. Her shaking eased, and I was oddly comfortable.

It didn't make any sense.

I pushed the lingering questions and thoughts away.

This kid had been through hell.

She was craving peace.

If being here with me was going to help give her that, then I wasn't going to question it.

Not anymore.

CHAPTER
22

It was later that night that I heard the bolt on the door disengage. Scarlett walked in with a box in her hands.

"I'll take that from you." I walked up to her, shifting the weight of the box into my hands.

It was surprisingly heavy.

"I have a ton of clothes in there. Taylor had some that she was getting around for our mom to donate. I didn't tell her much, just that I knew someone that needed them, so she told me to go ahead and take them."

"Thank you." I shifted the box in my hands and planted a kiss on her cheek. As I pulled away, she reached up and gently stroked my cheek. A slight hiss escaping between my teeth.

"Another fight?" There was a slight sting as her fingers brushed against the surface.

"Yeah, had to break up a fight last night." She moved her hand under my chin and pinched it gently with her finger and thumb.

"Need to tell that boss of yours, your face needs a vacation. You work too hard. That and he needs to give you a raise." I laughed. Her Dad took safe care of us, but she had a clever idea, a vacation sounded great. She let go of my face and looked down the hallway. "Where is she?"

"She's in the living room." We walked toward the living room, and I set the box down on the kitchen table. Scarlett had stopped next to the couch, and they were looking at each other.

"Scarlett, this is Katie. Katie, this is my girl-friend, Scarlett. Her Dad owns the bar down-stairs." Katie reached out her hand and shook Scarlett's.

"It's nice to meet you," Scarlett said. Katie nod-ded her head.

"She doesn't talk." Scarlett tilted her head, her eyes filling with tears when she saw the bruising on Katie's neck. She put her hand to her mouth and turned to me. Her eyes glistening as they were illuminated by the kitchen light behind me. I put my hands on her arms and rubbed them gently.

"It's okay. She's going to be okay." I said quietly. She closed her eyes and nodded. Before sniffling and pushing the tears back. She turned to Katie and smiled.

"Can I sit with you?" Katie nodded and Scarlett took a seat on the couch. The tv was on, but I only had Netflix, and Katie was trying to find some-thing to watch. I watched them interact with each other. When Katie landed on a title of interest she looked at Scarlett, waiting for her approval.

"Have you seen this one?" Scarlett asked. Katie shook her head no.

"It's a good one, go ahead and turn it on." Katie nodded and pushed the play icon. The title appeared across the screen, Love Again. I rolled my eyes. Another chick flick, one that Scarlett had insisted we watched a while ago. I did get through it and will admit it was a good movie, but I was more of an action guy.

They were entranced by the movie as I sipped a cup of coffee in the kitchen. Watching over their shoulders. Scarlett seemed comfortable after sitting with Katie for a while. Looking at the time, I had to get to the bar. I put my cup down and walked up behind the couch, putting my hands on Scarlett's shoulders. She turned her head upwards towards me and smiled.

"I have to go to work." She looked at Katie and then back at me.

"I'm going to stay and hang out with Katie."

I couldn't place it, but for some reason her words removed a tension.

One I hadn't realized was weighing on me.

"Okay, well I'll be downstairs if either of you need me." I leaned down and kissed her. She pulled away and smiled.

"I'll get you if either of us needs anything, but I think we will be fine. Girl's night, no boys, and an unlimited amount of chick flicks." Katie looked at Scarlett and smiled.

"Alright then, well I'm off."

"Have a good night. Don't get into any fights."

"I'll do my best," I laughed slightly and then headed down the hallway. Walking out, I heard the movie start to play once more, closing the door behind me, I locked it, before heading down to the bar, the sounds from the apartment dissipating as I got closer to the outer door.

When I walked in Jared was already sitting at the bar waiting. We didn't open for about fifteen minutes. He stood and walked over when he saw me walking in from the back door.

"Did you make sure it was locked this time?"

"Yes. We won't have any surprise visitors tonight."

"Did you get things figured out with that girl?"

"Her name is Katie."

"What ended up happening to her?"

"She is in my apartment, watching movies with Scarlett."

"She's back early?"

"Yeah."

"How did she take it?"

"She wasn't happy about it at first, but she came back this evening with some clothes for Katie and now they are hanging out."

"So, she's staying with you?"

"For now." Jared shook his head.

"I don't know, man. It's all bizarre."

"She's scared. She's all alone."

"She doesn't have anyone?"

"Not that I know of. Her parents are gone and so is her brother."

"Think she's a system kid then?"

"It's possible."

"So, the police might be looking for her."

"Possibly."

"What are you going to tell them when they come knocking?"

"The truth. She can only communicate through writing. I'm saving everything so that way when the time comes to involve the police or they come around, I can give it to them and maybe they can really help her."

"Why aren't you doing that now?"

"She wasn't born this way; someone made her this way. Her voice was stolen from her when she was attacked."

"Why didn't the police step in?"

"I'm willing to bet that she didn't have time to get help. There was blood on her clothes. This was recent." Jared sighed heavily and rubbed his eyes with his hands as he shook his head.

"That's fucked up."

"Yeah it is."

"What are you going to do?" I sighed as I walked over and leaned against the bar.

"I don't know."

"Well, whatever you decide to do, you might want to do it soon, before things get ugly." I nodded.

It was a little while later into the shift, Jared had joined me inside and together we threw several people out as things were getting crazy, when I felt my phone vibrate in my pocket. Pulling it free, I saw the text message was from Scarlett.

"Did you know your Dad was coming?" I looked up from the phone.

"What is it?" Jared asked.

"A text from Scarlett, she said my Dad's in town." Looking back at the screen my fingers tapped ferociously as I replied.

"No. Did he see Katie?"

"No. I caught him going up the stairs when I got back." I began to type again when I deleted it and called her. She answered the call on the second ring.

"You left her alone?" I asked, without even saying hello, my concern at the moment was that Katie had been left alone and now my Dad was for some reason in town.

"Just for a moment to run to the store." Her voice was shaky.

"Are you okay?"

"Yeah, I came down to the bar, but it was getting pretty rowdy. Daddy threw me out."

"As he should have. You know it's not safe."

"I know." I swallowed hard, the memory of why she wasn't really allowed in the bar anymore raising its head, bringing back things I would rather forget.

"Are you sure, you're okay?"

"Yes. I was just startled when I came back and found your Dad, walking up the stairs to the apartment."

"Is Katie okay?"

"Yeah, she's fine. I don't think she knows what happened." I looked at Jared as he studied me questioningly.

"What did he say?"

"He said he was looking for you." I could hear something in her voice, like she was crying.

"He say why?"

"No. Just that he was." I looked around the bar and saw the door open, walking in was my father.

"He just walked in. I'll call you back. Just remember to lock the bottom door, especially at night."

"That's the thing, babe." She stopped. I could hear her exhale, the unmistakable tremor relaying in her voice. "I did." I felt a lump rise in my throat at her words.

"I'll call you back." I hung up the phone as he approached me. He clapped my shoulder.

"Hello, son." Unease crawled up my spine at his touch. We were never close after the accident, and my mom had told me when I had gotten home that we had been estranged before it happened. Even with his attempts to get me to warm up to him after, I still had a residual desire to keep him at a safe distance.

"Hi, Dad. What are you doing here?"

"I thought I would stop by and see how you were settling in."

"It's been good, things are a little busy right now though." Almost on cue a chair hit the back wall. Jared moved in that direction, eyeballing me as he did.

"Sounds like it," Dad replied.

There was something in his tone.

Accusatory.

Like he knew something and was setting me up.

To catch me in a lie.

A trap.

"Look, now really isn't a good time."

"I understand, son, you're working."

"Are you going to be in town for a bit?"

"Just a few days."

"Okay, we can grab dinner, say tomorrow or Monday."

"Monday, sounds perfect, I'll be at the Conrad." I nodded and headed off in the same direction as Jared.

When I reached Jared, he already had the situation handled. I turned my head towards the door and saw my Dad's back as he disappeared into the crowded street.

"What was that about?" Jared asked.

"I have no idea."

He'd only come out once.

Months ago.

No call.

No warning.

It felt strange.

Threatening.

My eyes stayed on the door as it closed, locking the waiting crowd back outside.

His visit couldn't have come at a worse time.

CHAPTER
23

When I walked in, Scarlett's tear-filled eyes snapped to me, fear etched across her face.

My heart fell into my stomach.

"What's wrong?" I asked as I quickly made my way down the hall. Scarlett swiveled her head back towards the kitchen.

"Katie!" She disappeared through the entryway. My footsteps fell heavily as I ran down the hallway. Rushing in behind her, I joined Scarlett next to Katie, who was writhing on the floor, unable to breathe. I picked her up carrying her into the living room. Placing her gently on the couch I nudged her.

"Katie?" Her lips were parted and there were strangled gasps coming from between them. I looked back at Scarlett.

"Where's the inhaler?"

"I don't know, I looked for it on the table, but it wasn't there."

I dropped to my knees, reaching under the couch where it must have fallen.

My fingers brushed plastic. I gripped it tight.

"Got it." I pulled the cap off and stuck it in her mouth, pushing down on the plunger.

"Come on Katie," Scarlett begged. I gently shook her arm, waiting patiently for a response.

When the strong gasp came from her lips, I exhaled a sigh of relief. Scarlett scooped Katie up into her arms and hugged her tightly.

After Katie fell asleep, Scarlett and I sat in the kitchen, a pot of coffee steaming in the quiet.

"What happened?"

"We were sitting in the kitchen, and she had fallen asleep. I woke her up and she fell back out of the chair." Her voice trembled as she recalled what had transpired and I reached across the table and took her hand as she fell silent.

"You can go to bed if you want, babe. I can stay up with her," I said quietly. Scarlett stood with a sigh as she held her head in her hands, pacing around in the small space. She was shaken and watching her, I could tell that there was more going on that what had happened with Katie. My father showing up unannounced was sure to have played a role and then this on top of it. She walked over to the counter and prepared two cups of coffee. Returning to the table, she sat one of them in front of me and the other where she had been sitting.

"No, it's my fault, I'll stay up with you."

"You didn't do anything; you just tried to wake her up."

"She could have died, Sam." Her voice quivered.

"But she didn't. She is going to be okay." Scarlett sat back in the chair and hugged herself tightly, running her hands up and down her arms.

"I had a nightmare," she said softly. My cup was in midair, and I quickly put it back down. My mind racing.

"Was it him?" I asked, a growl rising in my chest. She nodded.

"What did he do?"

Scarlett looked toward the living room.

"He killed Katie."

"Why would she be in your dream?" My question tossed me back into my own dream from the night before, how Katie was there, but I didn't know why.

"I don't know." My thoughts snapped back to Scarlett. The tears in her eyes began to stream down her face rapidly and I reached out, cupping her face in my hands and swiping them away.

"It was just a dream; he can't hurt you or Katie. Alright?" She nodded and a yawn escaped her. I sighed as I stood to get more coffee. When I turned around, Scarlett's head was resting on her arms on the table.

"Babe?" She didn't respond. That was fast. A slight chuckle escaped me as I put the cup down and hoisted her up out of the chair and carried her to the bedroom.

After getting Scarlett settled for the night, I returned to the kitchen and grabbed my cup of coffee. Walking into the living room I sat down in the chair. Katie slept soundly on the couch, snuggled under the blanket. A chill ran through the room, and I quivered. Taking the cup in both hands, letting it warm them.

When I woke up, Scarlett was in the kitchen. Katie was still sleeping. I quietly got up from the chair, picking up my empty mug and entered the kitchen.

"When did I go to bed?" Scarlett asked.

"I carried you in about four thirty."

"What's the plan for today?" I grimaced slightly at her question.

"I have to go do inventory with your Dad this morning."

"Do you think Katie would like to go shopping?"

"You could ask her."

It wasn't long before Katie walked into the kitchen. Scarlett was talking to her about going shopping when I walked back to the bedroom to grab clothes. As I pulled clean clothes out, I pulled an envelope from my dresser drawer. I had been saving some money for an emergency but figured I could send it with the girls in case Katie wanted something. I pulled a thick stack of bills from the envelope and placed it on the nightstand.

After I left the bathroom, I walked into the kitchen. I grabbed my travel mug from the sink and began to fill it. Scarlett and Katie nowhere in sight, probably getting ready.

The sound of the liquid gold pouring into my cup was overshadowed by shifty footsteps. My eyes looked up as I saw her out of my peripheral.

Scarlett, her arms wrapped around her tightly. I put the cup down and reached for her.

"What's wrong?"

"She has a scar." She hesitated. "Like from a bullet."

"What?" I felt the panic in my voice as I reached out and pulled her hands from her sides, holding them tightly.

"She was doing her hair, and I saw it, she has a gunshot scar on her left side." My eyes glanced out into the empty hallway, before returning to her.

"Did it look recent?"

"It's healed, but it was dark, kind of like." Her voice failed her and her eyes drifted to her arm.

I knew full well what lay hidden underneath the sleeve. I gently took her chin and her eyes flicked to mine.

"I will never, ever let anything like that happen again. To you or Katie." It was more than a promise, a vow that I intended with my very life to keep. I would do whatever it took to protect them, come what may.

Scarlett smile slightly, pushing through the tears.

"You girls have fun today." She nodded. I grabbed my coffee cup and kissing her cheek softly.

"See you after."

I was walking down the hallway when Katie emerged from the bathroom.

"You look nice," I said, tousling her hair. A ghost of a memory flared and vanished before I could grab it. She turned and playfully swatted at me. I raised my hands, one holding my travel mug full of coffee.

"Grass or gravel, kid, you pick." The words flew from my lips.

Unfamiliar.

Her eyes immediately widened.

She turned into Scarlett and hugged her tightly as she began to cry.

"I didn't mean to scare her."

"I don't think it's that," Scarlett said. My heart dropped when she then mouthed the word 'brother' over Katie's head. It wasn't bad enough that I reminded her of him, I teased her probably as he used to.

"You two have fun today." My voice was quiet. Scarlett nodded as she rubbed Katie's back. I headed to the door and walked out, making my way to the bar for inventory.

It was about an hour after I got to work that I remembered the laundry that needed done, including Katie's clothes.

"Alec, is it okay if I do laundry today?" He turned from his count and nodded. "I'll be right back." I headed out of the back room and towards the back door.

When I reached the apartment the girls were already gone. I walked into my room and grabbed the laundry basket and headed downstairs with it.

At the washer in the back room of the bar, I began pulling things out, fixing them so they washed right. I pulled Katie's muddy jeans out and flipped them, shaking them, I heard something fall out of one of the pockets and hit the floor. I threw the pants in the washer and bent down to grab it. It looked like a card. When I flipped it over, my mouth went dry. It was a Virginia driver's license, with Katie's picture but not her name.

"Isabel Twain?"

I flipped the card over and back again.

It was real and her name wasn't Katie.

Anger gripped my chest as I read it over and over again.

The license thudded in my palm.

She'd lied.

But why?

I pulled my phone from my pocket and dialed Scarlett's number, but it rang through to voice-mail. If she had lied to me about who she was, what else had she lied about?

I was in the back with Alec when we heard the door open and then shut again. I walked out of the back to find Scarlett and Katie, or not Katie with shopping bags in their hands. Rage roared through my veins at the sight of this mystery girl I had taken in. I walked forward, my heart pounding, taking Scarlett's arm and pulling her behind me. I glared at this girl, and her eyes were instantly fearful.

"Who are you?" I yelled.

"Babe, what are you doing?" Scarlett tried to go around me, and I blocked her with my arm.

"Tell me."

Katie. Isabel. Whoever she was shuddered under my glare, taking a step back.

I threw the ID on the floor. The snapping sound echoing through the bar. She looked down. Staring at it as the face of the girl on the license stared back at her.

With pleading eyes, she looked up at me.

"GET OUT."

She stumbled, slamming against the door.

Her eyes, bright blue, riddled with terror.

Another flash in the back of my mind made my heart drop.

She turned, opening the door.

And was gone.

"Sam what the hell?" Scarlett asked. I leaned down and picked up the ID and handed it to her. She took it and a gasp of shock came from her lips.

"It's her," she said.

"What do you mean?"

"That's Isabel, the girl from Virginia. She's in danger."

"She lied to us."

"Sam, she's a scared girl. The Virginia police have been looking for her; she truly is in danger." Before I could stop her she darted out the door.

"Isabel!" I heard her calling as she ran down the street.

"Scarlett." She didn't come back. In my rage, I turned and trudged back into the back room. Alec looked at me as I entered.

"What's going on?"

"Nothing," I grumbled. My body shook with anger, how could I have been so trusting. She lied to me about everything.

It wasn't much later that I heard the door open and close again. Stewing I shook my head; I wasn't going out there. My guilt was creeping in; I shouldn't have yelled at her like that.

She's just a kid.

A scared kid.

"I'll be right back," Alec said. I nodded and continued counting. My mind wandered to Isabel's face as I threw the ID down on the floor.

The fear in her eyes.

It was almost like a shock went through me in that moment and there was a pair of similar eyes in the back of my mind.

I pushed it away and kept counting.

"Sam!"

My mind snapped free when Alec called. I rushed out front, the clipboard hitting the floor as I saw Scarlett lying there, blood pooling from her leg while Alec pressed a towel to it.

"Baby? Baby?" Her head lolled back into the curve of my arm, and I felt a sudden burst of familiarity. "Call nine one-one!" Alec fished his phone from his pocket. His voice was muffled as I focused on Scarlett.

"Sam?" Her voice was weak.

"Baby, can you hear me?" She groaned slightly. I looked up at Alec. "Tell them to hurry." He nodded and continued talking to them on the phone.

When the paramedics arrived, they quickly came in.

"Step back please," one of them addressed me. I let go of Scarlett and they replaced me gently, laying her flat on the floor. She had stopped shaking minutes ago, but her chest was still moving. I looked down at my hands, her blood on them, staining them. There was another flash in the back of my mind that made me wince. Within minutes they loaded Scarlett up. Alec jumped into the back of the rig.

"I'll meet you at the hospital," I said. He nodded and the ambulance took off. I rushed around the bar, shutting lights off, grabbing my keys. I headed out the door and locked it. Turning around I came face to face with four men.

"We're closed," I said breathlessly. The man before me stood looking tired, disheveled, and worn. I was in a hurry and tried to go past him. He shook his head for a minute and then opened his mouth to speak. I looked at the faces of the others with him, and they were looking at me the same way.

"What?" I asked irritated. The man held up a picture.

"Have you seen this girl?"

I practically ripped the picture from his hand. Anger surged when I saw her face staring back at me.

I was angry.

About her lies.

Scarlett being injured.

It was her fault.

No.

It was mine.

I had let her into our lives.

Letting her injuries sink the hooks that would pull my world apart.

Before I could think, I hauled back and hit him. Blood arced from his nose. He had a hard face.

"What the fuck?" A man with long black hair stepped forward and the man I had hit held his hand up despite being doubled over in pain.

"A no would have been fine," he groaned.

"You stay the hell away from her. I saw the damage you did to her, you sick son of a bitch. Don't think for a minute that I would ever let you get near her." He snapped up almost immediately.

The words that came.

I had felt rage before, but that...

That was the most I had ever felt.

Where the hell did that come from?

"What are you talking about?" I held the picture up to him.

"Her." He reached out, his hand bloody, taking the picture back and flipping it back towards me. Blood smeared on the side of the photo.

"This is my daughter, Isabel. She's missing." I looked at him again and the man next to him, placed his hand on his shoulder.

"He's telling the truth. I'm his brother, this is my niece we are searching for, she went missing three days ago." The man I had hit was still bleeding profusely and anxiety ran through my chest when I thought about getting to Scarlett.

I had no idea where Isabel had gone.

I was too preoccupied to ask.

"I am on my way to the hospital. I have to go."

"I just need to know if you have seen her, which by your reaction I would say you have." I could feel my chest heaving as I stared into his eyes, they held a hidden hope as he awaited my answer.

"I have."

"Where is she?" She never came back with Scarlett, and I still had no idea what had happened.

"I don't know." My heart dropped into my stomach. What the fuck had happened out there when Scarlett went after her? Had Isabel hurt her? My stomach began to turn, and I knew that it wouldn't settle until I got to Scarlett and got answers. "I bet that I can find out, but I really have to get to the hospital."

"We will follow you there." There was an uneasiness inside me that followed his words, but I didn't have time to argue. I nodded and ran around to the alley to retrieve my car.

CHAPTER
24

When we arrived at the hospital, the man was still bleeding and was intending to get checked out to make sure I didn't break his nose. He was probably going to file a report against me as well, but that didn't matter. I had to find Scarlett.

Rushing in the door, I found Alec sitting in the waiting room, blood on his shirt. He held his head in his hands.

"Alec?" He looked up at me and there was something in his eyes that I couldn't quite discern.

"She's going to be okay."

"What happened to her?"

"She was shot." As the words reached my ears, they distorted. "Someone shot her." A voice no longer his, echoing from rain and gunfire that didn't belong to the moment.

I blinked.

"By whom?"

"She didn't say." I looked from him to the nurse at the desk and walked over. My heart pounding with every step that I took.

"How can I help you?" she asked.

"I need to see Scarlett Wagner." She tapped away on her screen.

"She was just taken back from x-ray. Let me check with the doctor and see if she can have any visitors." I nodded and she disappeared.

It felt like an eternity before she came back.

"They are getting ready to repair the wound, it could take about an hour, if you don't mind waiting." I shook my head.

"Has she said anything yet? Did she say who did this to her?"

"That I don't know." I nodded and went back to take a seat with Alec. Sitting down, the men that had been with the other guy were sitting nearby waiting for him to come out of triage. I leaned over to the one with the long black hair.

"I'm sorry, I misunderstood."

"Why did you hit him?"

"Katie." I stopped myself, remembering that wasn't her name. "Isabel, I guess, told me her name was Katie and that she was running from someone. Someone who had attacked her, but she didn't say who."

"How did she end up with you?" he asked.

"She showed up at the bar where I work." I felt a chill run down my spine as I recalled that night when I first saw her and she was covered in bruises.

"She was attacked but not by him, that man loves her more than life itself." My thoughts ran across the last few days.

"Was the brother thing real?"

"What do you mean?"

"She told me her brother died."

"Yeah, he did."

"What happened to him?"

"He died saving her."

"From what?"

"Drowning." My body locked at his words. This poor girl had really been through it, but I couldn't imagine what she could have done to have people out there wanting to kill her. Something struck deep down inside of me; the sound of rain and thunder plagued my mind.

"Sam?" I looked up and the nurse from the window was standing in the doorway.

"Yes?" I got to my feet quickly.

"Scarlett is asking for you." I looked back at the guy I was sitting next to and nodded. He silently returned a nod, as I got up and began heading in her direction.

When I entered the room, she was sitting up in bed.

"Babe?" Her eyes immediately filled with tears.

"Baby, you have to find her."

"What do you mean?"

"Isabel."

"What happened, baby? Did she do this to you?" I put my hand on her head, smoothing her hair.

"No, of course not. I tried to save her, but I couldn't."

"What are you talking about?"

"He was there when I got there."

"Who?"

"He took her, and I tried to stop him, that's when he shot me." My heart shattered when the words left her mouth, floating into the air. My mind began to run rampant.

Had the person who attacked her finally caught up?

"Who? Who took her?" She squeezed her eyes shut and covered her mouth with her hand as she tried to suppress a deep sob.

She shook her head.

She didn't know.

Tears fell relentlessly down her face.

"It's going to be okay. I'm going to find her." She opened her eyes and nodded.

"Go." It wasn't a request; it was a plea. I nodded and kissed her hard on the lips.

As I pulled the door open, I turned back to her.

"I love you," I said.

"I love you, too."

"I'll be back."

"Babe, there's something you need to know." I shut the door slightly so no one else could over-hear her.

"What is it?"

"My Dad knew."

I froze. The words didn't register at first, like a bad connection.

"What do you mean?"

"He knew that she was staying with you."

"How?"

"I called and asked him to help her."

I felt tension coiling in my stomach.

I wasn't angry with her.

She was trying to help.

I turned towards the door.

"Sam?"

I didn't turn; my eyes locked like my hand on the handle.

"He sounded familiar."

"What do you mean?"

I turned my eyes locking with hers. Tears in them, said what she couldn't.

Shock racked my body.

As I walked back out into the waiting room, the four men from the bar were talking, while Alec sat in a chair close by.

"Sam? How's Scarlett?"

"She's going to be okay. I have to go."

"Where are you going?"

"The man that shot her, took Isabel."

"Who did it?"

"Scarlett didn't say." I took a deep breath before I spoke again. "She said you knew." Alec's eyes dimmed as he stood.

"She called me and asked me to help her."

"Did you tell anyone she was here?" I looked at him, and his shoulders fell slightly. He had told someone. "Who?" He shook his head and looked at me, locking his eyes with mine.

"A man would do anything to protect his children."

His words hit something in me I didn't understand.

Not yet anyway.

I felt the blood in my veins running cold, time was running out.

"We can deal with that later, right now I have to find Isabel."

"I'm so sorry," Alec said as he turned his attention back to the man I had hit earlier.

"I'll deal with you later, after I get my daughter back. If she's hurt because of you." He stopped. His voice was laced with anger and my heart felt for him. I could never imagine what it would be like to go through what he was going through.

Losing his son.

Possibly his daughter as well.

"I have to go," I said.

"I'm coming with you," the man said. I cocked an eyebrow at him. "She's my daughter." We stared at each other for a moment; there was an unrelenting determination in his eyes, he wasn't going to take no for an answer. The moment was suddenly broken as his phone began to ring loudly from his pocket.

"One minute." I nodded, walking away to make my own phone call.

The phone rang a few times and was answered by a pleasant voice on the other side.

"Thank you for calling The Conrad, how can I be of assistance today?"

"I was calling to get the room number for William Milier." I had to call my Dad and let him know that we wouldn't be at dinner tomorrow. I wasn't going to make Scarlett sit through a dinner with my estranged father, after being shot in the street, a block away from me.

"I'm sorry, we don't have any guest checked in under that name." I felt the recoil in my stomach at her words. It wouldn't surprise me if he just got up and left and went back to California. He was flighty.

The man didn't even have a cell phone.

"Alright, thank you."

"You're welcome." The call ended and I returned to the small group of men. The man had also finished his phone call and was filling the others in. He ran his hand over his face. His distress evident.

"We should get moving," I said as I approached them. The man sighed heavily and put his hands on his hips, nodding.

"Let's go." His voice was steady.

The tables had suddenly flipped.

We were now the hunters.

CHAPTER
25

When we got back to the bar, I led the group down the alleyway to my apartment. Unlocking the door, I jerked my head toward the stairs signaling for them to come up. As we entered the kitchen, I leaned against the counter, crossing my arms over my chest. I had no idea how we were going to find her or who had taken her.

"Where do we even start?" My eyes drifted over to the shorter kid; he had to be about eighteen years old.

"We have nothing to help us find Katie."

"Isabel." He corrected me. I looked at him briefly and nodded.

"Got it," the man said. He was looking at his phone. I straightened myself and walked over to him.

"What is it?"

"Camera footage of the street." He played it back for me and there was a black car. A man was pulling on Isabel; she slipped free reaching for Scarlett. Then he raised his gun. I looked away. The flash from the screen catching in my peripheral. I couldn't watch.

"How did you get that video?" I asked as my stomach began to turn.

"I have connections." I nodded, I really didn't need to know how he had gotten it, but I needed to know how it was going to help us.

"We should inform the police."

"No."

My eyes locked with his.

"They will kill her."

"They can go in quiet." He shoved the phone back in his pocket.

Within a breath, we were chest to chest.

Desperation radiating from him.

"This isn't a game. This is my daughter's life."

I relented, stepping back.

He knew the situation far better than I did.

But I wasn't a stranger to the stakes.

"Then we should get going." I wanted to get out there; I wanted to find her as much as they did. It was my fault she was in this position in the first place; I shouldn't have yelled at her the way I did.

"I'm waiting to get more details about the car and where it went. There are cameras all over this city." I was curious as to how he knew that, remembering that his daughter's license was from Virginia.

"You know a lot about Nashville."

"We used to live here. For Isabel's entire life until we moved over a year ago."

"*We're moving.*" The voice came to me clearly from somewhere in the dark of my memory that I couldn't access. I shook my head.

I had to focus.

She hadn't lied to me about that.

She really was from here, just not currently.

"What happened to your face?" My mind shifted away from my thoughts as I looked at him, his eyes held a curiosity as they settled on the scar on my face.

"I was in a motorcycle accident a little over eight months ago."

"Where are you from?"

"California."

"How did you end up in Nashville?" The question caught me off guard. Nashville was a booming city with plenty of jobs, and I wanted to start over after the accident. There was so much more to it than that, that I had never said out loud.

"I don't know how to explain it. I feel connected to it somehow and my Dad encouraged me to move; he set me up with a job at the bar and this apartment."

"Do you remember anything from your accident?"

"Not really."

"Why did you take my daughter in?"

"She found me when she made it into the bar Friday night. I tried to send her away, but she was terrified and had obviously been injured. I didn't have the heart to send her away, so I was still trying to figure out what happened before I involved anyone else." My heart fell into my stomach, as I recalled my harsh reaction when I found out she had lied to me about who she was. All of this may have been avoided if I had just controlled my anger and not thrown her out. I clamped my eyes shut and her terrified blue eyes appeared.

"I can never thank you enough for all that you did for her." I opened my eyes locking with his. My gut twisting into knots.

Don't thank me yet.

"We should start looking," I said. In that moment, his phone went off in his hand, and he glanced down at it.

"They headed East, out of town." He began to make his way towards the door, and we followed him. I turned back as they headed back downstairs, grabbing a piece of paper off the pad that Isabel had used. I turned it over and scribbled my phone number down.

Outside, they had gotten into the truck, and I rushed over and handed the man the paper.

"This is my number in case you find anything," I said. He nodded and quickly put the number into his phone, and then I felt my phone vibrate.

"Now you have mine as well." I pulled the phone from my pocket and the name Michael Twain appeared on the caller ID.

"Got it."

It was just after midnight, I was leaning against my car, filled with questions and enough anger to pulverize something, when the headlights of Mike's truck washed over me, and they pulled in. They got out and approached me.

"Did you find anything?" Mike asked.

"No, you?"

"Nothing."

"It's like they completely vanished." I put my hands on my head as my chest tightened.

"Have you tried to call your contact again, to see if they have any new information?"

"They are digging, but they aren't finding anything."

"Can't they track the car? It should have a GPS."

"It's disconnected."

"So, there's nothing left." It came out quietly as the realization hit me.

Dreaded silence filled the space.

"Dammit!" He yelled, his voice cracking against the night as he kicked an abandoned beer can.

Aluminum scraped against the concrete, skidding across ice.

"Calm down, Mikey," the other man said. It was obvious they were brothers as they shared the same jawline, and their noses were practically identical.

"How can I? She is out there with God knows who and Solomon is going to walk free."

"Solomon?" I asked.

I had heard that name before.

It filled me with an indescribable dread.

Unfamiliar.

Like a far darker shadow in the dark.

Lingering.

Mike quickly turned.

"Do you know him?"

His voice hoarse.

Laced with fear.

Anxiety.

"No. But the name sounds familiar."

He turned away from me and pulled his phone from his pocket. He wandered back towards the truck as the rest of us remained.

"You have to understand, this is really hard for him, especially since you." The other man stopped.

"Remind him of his dead son? Yeah, Isabel said I reminded her of him too." The words flew out of my mouth faster than I intended and he nodded solemnly.

"It's been hard on everyone since he died."

"What was he like?" I asked.

"He was really smart, a sweet kid." He stopped peering over at Mike as he spoke on the phone, he turned back to me. "He loved that little girl more than anything." My heart ached at his words. It all made sense now, Isabel felt comfortable because I reminded her of him. The teasing in the hall-way and her immediate reaction came to mind. I palmed my face and the image of me tousling her hair appeared. I sighed heavily.

"Well, I don't know much about what happened, but I can tell you that I will do whatever I can to help you guys get Isabel back." He smiled slightly.

"Thank you." My eyes turned to the other two who were with him. I noticed what they were wearing which was far from the appropriate attire for this time of year.

"Where are you guys from?" I asked.

"Hawaii."

"Why the hell are you in Nashville?"

"To help find Isabel. She's our friend and I promised her that we would be there for her no matter what."

"What are your names?" I asked, completely forgetting my manners earlier in the hospital.

"I'm Sitka and this is my brother Keone." I shook each of their hands.

"And I'm Ben, Mike's brother." I shook his hand as well.

"I'm sorry if I was rude by not asking earlier, there was a lot going on in the moment."

"Don't worry about it, we didn't exactly ask either," Ben replied with a slight chuckle. Just then Mike began to walk quickly back towards us.

"Load up guys, we are going back to the house."

"What about Isabel?" Keone asked.

"There's nothing we can do tonight. We will have to pick up again tomorrow." I watched his face turn and then he took off back towards the truck. The sound of vomiting echoed into the quiet night.

"Mike?" Ben called.

"I'm okay," he yelled back.

"What is it?"

"Nothing, just give me a minute."

After a few minutes of standing in silence, Mike made his way back over.

"Let's go." His eyes met mine. "We will be back in a little bit." I nodded.

"I'll call you if I hear anything," I said. They turned to walk back to the truck, and I headed down the alleyway towards the apartment.

When I got upstairs, I pulled my phone from my pocket and immediately dialed Scarlett's number. It was a little after one in the morning, but I had been so busy helping them look for Isabel, that I didn't want to get her hopes up until I knew more, which even now I had no idea what was going on. She answered after the third ring.

"Hello?" Her sweet voice sounded tired.

"Hey baby, how are you feeling?"

"Like I was shot in the leg," she chuckled slightly as she tiredly responded. I felt my eyebrows furrow.

"Not funny."

"I'm kind of doped up at the moment." There was silence and then a gasp. "Did you find Isabel?"

Her voice seemed more alert with her question. I sighed.

"Not yet."

"Do you have anything?"

"No." I ran my hand over my face.

"Do you want me to come over and help?"

"Absolutely not. You need to rest. Did they release you?"

"Yes, they sent me home a while ago. I was going to call you, but I fell asleep as soon as I got into bed."

"Are you at your place or your parents?"

"Daddy, brought me to their house."

"Babe, can you think of who your Dad might have told that Isabel was here?"

"He said he was going to call a friend to help find out more about her and try to help."

"I'm just hoping whoever he called really was intending to help her and not hurt her."

"I know." I didn't know how we were going to go about it, but what Alec did made me question if he was trustworthy. He said he did it to protect his daughters but if that were true then he would have informed the police. He was hiding something; I didn't want to think these things of a man who treated me like his own son from the moment I set foot in the place.

Would he sell out a sixteen-year-old girl?

Our interaction lingered.

The little response he gave me didn't sit right.

"What's on your mind?" Her voice broke through my tumultuous thoughts.

"Nothing." I sighed. "I'm just glad that you're okay."

"I miss you," her voice was soft like she was falling back asleep.

"You rest and I'll call you in the morning."

"Mhm, I love you." She hummed.

"I love you, too." I sat in the silence for a moment until I heard her breathing softly on the other line.

She had fallen asleep.

I ended the call and put my phone on the charger.

I couldn't sleep as I laid in bed, my arms propping my head up as my thoughts ran wild. My thoughts turned to my call with the Conrad.

Where had he gone?

I picked up my phone and called the house.

He had to have made it home by now.

It rang, but no one answered.

"Hi, you've reached the Milier's we can't." I hung up.

Frustrated I put it down on the nightstand, there was no point in trying to get ahold of him, he was ignoring me. Probably because he had to go back for some business and didn't want to tell me he had to bail on me again. He would probably wait a few months and then call me to try and make up for it.

I rolled over onto my side, a groan escaping me as everything that was going on collided in my head.

Covering my face with my pillow, I squeezed my eyes tightly beneath the softness, trying to find sleep.

When I opened my eyes, I was staring up at a ceiling. It was clear right off that it wasn't the same ceiling I had fallen asleep under as there was an evident crack in mine. I sat up, finding myself on a couch in a living room that I didn't recognize. I heard footsteps across the floor above me and stared up as I followed them.

They began to approach the stairs.

Intently, I watched to see who was going to come down.

I saw the first foot fall and then the second.

A hand slid into view as they came down the banister with another step.

I could see light blonde hair, hanging loosely.

The sudden sound of glass shattering made me turn my head away from the stairs.

There was nothing there.

When I turned back, a dark figure launched at me.

I shot up, breathing heavily as I took account of my surroundings. The silence that had filled the room was disrupted as my phone lit up and began to ring. I mumbled curses under my breath as I immediately leaned over, grabbing it. I didn't even bother looking at the name on the screen, it could be Mike, I just hit the button and put it to my ear.

"Hello?" There was silence. "Hello?" I waited again as the silence lingered before I heard a familiar, gruff voice push through from the opposing line.

"The dark moon meets the solstice in the dead of winter."

PART FOUR

Scarlett

CHAPTER
26

I t wasn't long after Sam went off to work that I got up to make us snacks. Opening the cupboards, I was dismayed to see that Sam hadn't yet gone to the store. I walked back into the living room, leaning over the back of the couch, Katie turned her head to look up at me.

"Well, there isn't much for snacks." I looked at the clock and saw that there was still time to get down to the market just down the street.

"I'm going to go to the store to grab some stuff, do you want to go with me?" Katie looked at me and there was almost a flash of fear in her eyes as she vehemently shook her head no.

"Okay, well I'm going to run really quick, and I'll be right back." Katie nodded. Heading back into the kitchen, grabbing my purse from the counter I headed out the door. As I stepped out into the alleyway, I turned and locked the door behind me. With the click engaging, I strolled toward the bustling sidewalk.

As I was walking through the throngs of Saturday night drinkers, I kept thinking about what Sam had told me about Katie. She seemed extremely comfortable with him. A smile spread across my face; he was a comfortable guy to be around. My cheeks grew warm as I thought about the first time I had met him.

I had opened the door to the apartment as Daddy had asked me to take some cleaning stuff over for the new tenant. As I stepped in I unceremoniously tripped on the last step, the cleaning supplies flying out of the box onto the floor. He appeared out of the bathroom, wearing only a pair of basketball shorts. My cheeks hot with embarrassment as I clumsily got to my feet. His hair was wet, hanging over his eyes and he had a towel around his neck. His muscles flexed as he crossed his arms taking a deep breath, his bare chest broad and his arms looked as though they could break bones with a simple squeeze.

"Can I help you?" he asked. I began throwing the cleaning stuff back into the box. Reaching for a runaway roll of paper towels, his hand grazed mine as he reached for it. I looked up at him and our eyes met. Fumbling I grabbed the roll and threw it back into the box. Snapping straight up, I held the box out to him. He took it and a smirk played at the corner of his lips. Without a word, I backed up to the door, trying not to fall down the steps.

"I'm sorry." I walked out and closed the door behind me. That was our first time meeting, and I thought that was the end of it, until he started working at the bar.

He was enigmatic.

His first shift at Daddy's bar, I was bartending trying to make money for the next semester and he was broody.

Far from the playful man I had encountered before.

I remembered he tried to cover his face with his hair at first, afraid of what people might think of his scar. My mind bounced back to that conversation. We had closed the bar down and I was curious, so I poured him a drink and grabbed myself one before joining him at the counter.

He stiffened.

He seemed different from the person I met when I stumbled into the apartment.

"You going to be quiet your entire time here or are you going to talk?" I asked. He smirked slightly as he took a drink of his beer.

"Do you always just walk into someone's apartment?" I was taken aback, I was hoping for a lighthearted conversation, but this kid wasn't having it.

"I'm sorry, my Dad asked me to take some stuff up, he didn't say that you had already moved in, just that you would be soon." I grabbed my beer and went to get up from the seat.

"Depends, on what you want to know?" His voice was deeper than I anticipated, I took his response as an invitation and sat back down, placing my beer on the bar.

"Well, I'm curious to know why you try to hide your scar?" I took a sip of my beer, and he sighed heavily next to me.

"It looks weird."

"I think it looks pretty bad ass. Whoever did that to you, you probably fucked them up even worse."

His muscles flexed next to me. I thought maybe I had upset him, but he sighed.

"Not exactly. I'm sure you'll be surprised to learn, that this is my first bouncing gig."

"Really?"

"Yeah, I've never worked in a bar before."

"I see," I said. I was still waiting with patience for an answer about the scar on his face. His eyes traced to the corners, looking at me, my anticipation written on my face as he opened his mouth to speak.

"I was in an accident." His voice was hollow, and I felt guilt creeping up into my throat as I tried to swallow my beer.

"I'm sorry."

"My friends and I were riding, when a storm broke out of nowhere and we were trying to get back to the house, when a car ran a red light and hit me."

"That's awful."

"Yeah, well I survived it, mostly." He took another drink and set the empty glass down with a loud clink on the bar.

"What do you mean?"

"I don't remember anything. I only know what everyone else told me. My parents, mostly. Whatever friends I had at that time, never showed up for me, so I never heard it from them what had happened."

"And the driver?"

"Oddly enough, never heard anything about that either, my Dad just said that it was taken care of and that I didn't have to worry about it."

"How did you end up here in Nashville?"

"I don't know. I was sitting there one day, and I was reading an article about Nashville and felt compelled to come here. My Dad insisted on it after I brought it up, he thought that maybe a change of scenery would be good for me."

"Has it?" I finished my beer. "Been good for you I mean." He turned his gaze to mine and in the light I could see he was locked onto me.

He didn't do what most guys did.

Look me up and down like a conquest.

He held eye contact.

"I think so far, but then again I just got here." He turned his head, and I was startled by the sudden break in eye contact.

"Is that going to be all today miss?" I looked startled up at the cashier and then down at the few things that I had placed on the counter.

"Yes, thank you." He began to check me out.

There was something on the radio behind him. Catching my attention as I heard it.

Faint.

Curious.

"Can you turn that up a little bit?" I asked. He nodded and turned to the radio, turning it up so that I could hear it better.

"Virginia police are asking locals to keep their eyes open. Isabel Twain is described as five foot five, long blonde hair, was last heard from February tenth, by her father Mike Twain. Twain is believed to have traveled to the Nashville area from Virginia. If sighted, please contact the local authorities."

"Scary world we live in," the cashier said. I broke from the words of the radio, and it turned to incoherent background noise. He was handing me my bags.

"Yeah, it is," I replied flatly.

As I stepped back out into the crowded street my heart was pounding. The words racing through my mind from the radio.

What were the fucking odds?

Katie shows up from out of nowhere and now there's a plea for help locating a missing girl from Virginia.

She was endangered.

But what if she was the danger?

Clutching the bag, I raced back towards the apartment.

CHAPTER
27

Walking up to the bar, Jared was working the door, checking ID's. When he saw me he removed the rope and let me in despite the groan coming from those who were waiting in line. As I went to walk past him, he gently took my arm.

"Are you okay?"

"Yeah, where's Sam?"

"Inside somewhere." He looked at me again, trying to read my face. I could tell my face was giving him a reason to feel concerned. Jared had worked for my Dad since the day the bar opened. He always took care of the bartenders, like an older brother.

"Is the girl okay?" My heart lurched forward at his question. "Katie's fine." He looked away from me and into the bar.

"Be careful, it's been really rowdy tonight. I've already had to kick a few people out." I gently reached up and touched his arm.

"Thank you, Jared." He smiled slightly as he released my arm.

As soon as my feet broke the threshold, hands were on my shoulders, and I was being guided to the right towards the bar. Turning around I was met with a familiar face.

"Baby girl, what are you doing here?" He wrapped his arms around me.

"Hi, Daddy. I came to talk to Sam, have you seen him?"

"He was over by the pool tables a minute ago, dealing with a rowdy bunch."

"I really need to talk to him." Dad's eyes scanned the room and voices of drunkards began to elevate near the back of the bar.

"Now's not a suitable time; it's getting rough in here. You should go back upstairs and wait for him there."

"But Daddy it's."

"It can wait; your safety is what matters to me. That's why you don't work for me anymore. Not after that." He interrupted. My mind began to spiral at his words. I full well remembered that night. Sam was taking out the trash, Jared had called off, Bobbie had left the front door unlocked when she left. I was at the bar counting when a man came in, his eyes the only thing I could see. He pulled a gun and pointed it at me.

"Give me the money." I held my hands up shak-ily and nodded as tears flooded my eyes.

"Please, don't shoot." My voice quivered as I spoke.

"Do it now!" He yelled, raising the gun and firing a shot off into the ceiling. A scream escaped me as I jumped. He tossed a bag on the bar, and I scrambled to gather all the cash and put it into the bag, to get him out of here.

His gun trained on me.

I shook as I kept my head down, unable to see anything other than what was happening with my hands.

Suddenly a bang rang out.

Cutting through the tension as a burning sensa-tion began in my left arm, like it had been touched by a wrought hot iron.

I cried out and fell to my knees behind the bar. I pushed my back against the cooler, trying to see what was happening in the mirror with no luck. I reached over and pushed the silent alarm that

Daddy had installed after being robbed the summer prior. I could hear a struggle ensuing on the other side of the bar but dared not get up. There was the sound of metal scraping across the floor and grunting. Finally, everything was quiet aside from the approaching sirens.

"Scarlett?" He appeared from thin air, sweat beading his brow, blood coming from his lip. His eyes wide with what almost looked like shock, but something hidden made me believe he had seen something like this before.

"Sam?" I sobbed. He picked me up, cradling me against his chest as he walked out the front door. The street was lit up with flashing red and blue lights.

"She's been shot; I need help over here!" Sam yelled. I heard the wheels clacking on the sidewalk before he placed me on a gurney. He pulled away, but I reached out and took his hand.

"Don't go," I pleaded through tears. He grazed his lips against my knuckles.

"I wouldn't dream of it." He planted a kiss on my hand. It was later that the police had informed Dad that the man, had managed to disappear before they were able to apprehend him.

For a while after that I found it hard to sleep, his deep brown, nearly black eyes haunting my slumber. I numbly felt the burning sensation radiating through my arm as I remained in the memory.

The sound of shattering glass brought me back to the bar. Dad stared at me intently. The bullet had only grazed me, but the lasting mental effect it had on me was like being squeezed by a vice. Dad gently took my arm and led me to the door.

"It's not safe. Go." At the door, he passed me off to Jared, who pulled me out and closed the door behind me. He regarded me silently and I felt the tears that slipped down my cheeks. I nodded silently and he opened the rope, letting me exit.

Approaching the door, I grabbed the knob to enter the stairwell. When I pulled it open I was surprised to see someone just walking up the stairs. My heart stopped in my chest, Katie was upstairs alone, and I know I didn't lock the top door, we never did as long as the bottom was locked.

"Hello?" My voice echoed up the empty stairwell. Reaching the man, he turned around and smiled at me. His eyes met mine and I felt my chest heave as I immediately recognized his face.

"Hello, Scarlett."

CHAPTER
28

"Mr. Milier." The surprise in my voice was hard to hide. He walked down a few steps, stopping just before me.

"It's good to see you again," he said with a slight smile.

"What brings you here?" I was quite sure Sam hadn't told his folks about Katie. He rarely even mentioned them. In the five months that he had lived here, he didn't mention visiting them or talking to them, only stories from after the accident. I had met his Dad only once when he was in town for business. The three of us had gone to dinner.

He seemed nice.

Normal.

This meeting seemed cold.

Calculated.

Unnerving.

"I'm looking for Sam. Is he upstairs?" He nodded his head towards the door at the top of the steps.

"No. He's at work, at the bar right here outside this door." He nodded and cast another smile at me before slowly coming down the rest of the stairs. Each thud sending a shiver down my spine. I slid over to the wall in the narrow entryway, clutching the bag tightly to my chest. He reached for the knob and looked at me with another smile.

"Thank you." I nodded and he walked passed me, out the door. As it closed behind him, I quietly locked it. I was certain I had done so before

I left. My thoughts immediately gravitated away from the unusual encounter to Katie.

"Katie?" I called as I rushed up the stairs. My heart racing with every step, fumbling with my keys when I got to the door, dropping them, as it creaked open. She stood there, looking at me quizzically. When my eyes met hers she returned a look of uneasiness as she saw the distress in my eyes. My heart lifted.

I was simply happy she was safe.

She stepped aside as I hurried in, closing the door behind me and locking it. Turning from it, I wrapped my arms around her and pulled her into a hug. An exhale of relief leaving my chest as I fought back tears. Pulling away, I held her at arm's length. She held her thumb up, asking me if I was okay. I took a step back, leaning against the door, breathing heavily and nodded.

"I'm okay. Are you okay?" I asked. She nodded and then held her hand out, offering to take the bag from me. Seeing her, made all the questions I had dissipate. Though similar to the description, there's no way this could be the same girl from the radio. She disappeared down the hallway, I straightened and followed her.

Pulling my phone from my pocket, I texted Sam.

"Did you know your Dad was coming?" It went through and three little dots appeared right away.

"No. Did he see Katie?" My fingers flew across the face of the phone as I replied.

"No. I caught him going up the stairs when I got back." The dots appeared again and then quickly disappeared. The screen lit up with Sam's face, and I answered the call.

"You left her alone?" he asked.

"Just for a moment to run to the store." My voice shook.

"Are you okay?" His voice was soft, concerned.

"Yeah, I came down to the bar, but it was getting pretty rowdy. Daddy threw me out."

"As he should have. You know it's not safe."

"I know." My voice shook again, and I swallowed hard.

"Are you sure, you're okay?"

"Yes. I was just startled when I came back and found your Dad walking up the stairs to the apartment."

"Is Katie okay?"

"Yeah, she's fine." I looked down the hall to see if I could see her, but she was still out of sight.

"What did he say?"

"He said he was looking for you." I felt tears creeping into my eyes as I tried to keep my voice low and not scare Katie.

"Did he say why?"

"No. Just that he was." Sam was silent for a moment.

"I think he just walked in. I'll call you back. Just try to remember to lock the bottom door, especially at night."

"That's the thing, babe." I stopped the specific memory playing in my head.

My hand.

The knob.

The key.

The distinct click of the lock.

"I did." He grew silent but only briefly.

"I'll call you back." I nodded and the call ended. I pulled the phone away and put it back in my pocket, looking down the hall, Katie was waiting, she had already popped a bag of popcorn and was holding the bowl in her hands. I quickly dashed away tears from my eyes.

"What are we watching next?" My voice shook. She looked at me curiously and cocked her head sideways.

"I'm okay. Come on, let's pick another movie." I forced a laugh. She nodded and bounded into the living room, as I followed.

When I broke the threshold to the living room, she was sitting on the couch, proudly looking up at me as she had already pulled up a new title. I looked at it and then back at her.

"I don't think I've ever seen The Labyrinth before." She turned her gaze away from me, grabbing the paper and pen from the coffee table. I heard the faint scratching noises before she leaned back and held the pad out for me to read over the back of the couch.

"It was your mom's favorite?" I felt a pinch of sadness rise in my chest. She nodded and then turned back to put the paper down, pulling the bowl of popcorn close to her. Seating it on her crossed legs. I walked around the couch and sat down. Grabbing the blanket from the back, I draped it over our legs. She adjusted the bowl in her lap, and I reached over grabbing a handful.

"This better be good," I joked, nudging her with my elbow. She turned her head and smiled at me before she pressed the play button on the remote. As the movie started, her eyes were locked on the screen, while mine were locked on her.

There was no feasible way this girl was any danger.

She was in danger, that we knew for sure just looking at her, but there was no way she was the girl from Virginia. I sighed slightly and turned my attention to the screen as a girl appeared in a beautiful gown.

When the goblin king appeared, my heart caught in my chest. His voice reminded me much of the man that had shot me and more so of Sam's father. Our encounter in the hallway re-entered my mind, like a bad dream. I reached back and pulled my phone out of my pocket. Checking the time it was a little after midnight. Sam will be getting off in a few hours. I felt a shift next to me and Katie regarded me in her silence. I shook the phone in my hand before reaching over and putting it on the coffee table. I sat back and Katie leaned against me. I put my arm around her, and it reminded me of the movie nights my sister and I used to have before I moved out and started going to school. We used to do movie nights every Friday.

It wasn't much longer when I felt a weight shift as Katie was still leaning against me. I gently leaned my head down to look at her and found that she was sound asleep. Carefully, I moved myself out from underneath her, gently letting her rest against the back of the couch. There was a light sigh that came from her as she moved, maneuvering herself to the other end. I pulled the blanket up and fixed it over her. I curled my legs up close to me on my end, covering myself with part of the blanket.

Resting my head on my arm, I continued watching the movie.

CHAPTER
29

The sound of the door creaking open startled me from my sleep. Carefully, I got up as to not wake up Katie, who was still quietly sleeping. The tv had timed out and the screen was black, making the apartment appear all the darker. Shaking my phone the flashlight came on, and I used it to light my way out into the hallway.

"Sam?" Shining my light there was no one in the hallway and no response. I walked over to the

switch, flipping it, only to find there was no power. I slowly walked down towards Sam's room.
The door was ajar. Pushing it open I stepped in
to find that no one was there, and nothing was
disturbed. Walking back out I headed to the door
to check the lock. Reaching out, I pulled my hand
back as I was startled to see that the door was
cracked open, and the lock had been disengaged.
A muffled cry came from the living room. I instantly felt a cold chill run up my spine and I
doubled back down the hall.

"Katie?" My feet pounded the floor as I made
my way down the hallway, it seemed to stretch
farther the faster I tried to run.

Running into the living room, he popped up
as I reached the couch, my flashlight in his face,
his eyes gleaming with a sense of pride in them,
hidden behind that same mask he had worn that
night.

I looked away from him at Katie.

Her eyes wide.

His hands wrapped around her throat.

He quickly jumped up, and I watched as her lifeless body shift when he raised himself up. I shined the light, hoping to blind him when he charged me, a horrendous scream, escaping me as his hands grabbed me.

I felt hands on me and shot up. Breathing heavily, looking around frantically, I realized that the hands belonged to Katie. Her eyes were wide with terror as she sat on the floor next to the couch. Taking a shaky breath, I tried my best to smile.

"I'm okay." She stood and held her hands out to me. I took them and she helped me to my feet, before leading me into the kitchen. Pulling out a chair, she threw her head towards it, inclining me to sit. Taking the seat, she walked over to the cabinet and started rifling through it. My hands shook as I placed them over my face. I hadn't had nightmares about that man in a while. It was probably triggered by Daddy bringing it up. What bothered me more than anything about the night-mare wasn't the fact that he was in it.

But what he had done to Katie.

Her lifeless eyes and the way her body shifted.

I squeezed my eyes tightly willing for the images to go away.

She wasn't there when this happened.

Yet she was in this nightmare.

My mind was a flurry when I heard something sliding across the table at me. Looking up, Katie was taking a seat across from me, a mug in her hand. My eyes cast down at the mug in front of me. The smell of the hot cocoa permeated the air and somehow relaxed my chaotic mind. I heard scribbling and looked up as Katie slid me a pad of paper.

"What's wrong?" I took the mug in my hands and felt the warmth residually spread throughout my body.

"Did you make cocoa?" I diverted the question. She took the pad back and scribbled again.

"Something my brother used to do for me when I had nightmares." I felt tears welling in my eyes as I read it. I looked up at her and her eyes exuded sadness.

"You must miss him terribly." She dashed away a stray tear and nodded her head before she took a sip from the steaming mug.

I pulled the mug to my lips, as the delicate hot chocolate touched my tongue a hint of something familiar danced on my tastebuds. I pulled it away swallowing.

"Did you add something to this?" She nodded and grabbed the pen and paper and scratched something out before turning it to me.

"Cinnamon and powdered sugar." She nodded.

"Where did you learn that?" I took a sip again, studying the warm liquid. I definitely recognized it. She scratched again.

"My mom." Reading what she wrote had me taken aback.

"I thought you told Sam that your mom had died?" She nodded solemnly and turned her gaze back to the cup in her hands, releasing one hand she took the pen and scribbled on the paper.

"She passed in a car accident." I peered over the edge of the mug, reading her words.

"I'm sorry, Katie." I reached across the table and held out my hand. She looked up and gently took it, and I squeezed it softly. "You are going to be okay." She nodded and I let go. I held the cup in both my hands again and studied her silently. She was a good kid; she just had a rough go of things. I heard my voice in my head as I told Sam that she wasn't our problem, but after spending some time with her, I wanted to help her with whatever I could. She needed to get out of the situation she was in. Sam was right if she went back she might not survive next time. An idea sparked in me, and I got up from the table. Katie looked at me quizzically.

"I'll be right back." She nodded and I headed into the living room.

Picking up my phone, I checked the time. We had only been asleep for less than an hour. Shaking the remnants of the dream away as they rose again I dialed the number. I knew I should discuss it with Sam first, but it was important and if something was going to be done to help Katie, it needed to be done fast. I would explain it all to him later and he would understand. I only wanted to help her.

Holding the phone to my ear, I peered out into the kitchen, to see Katie still sitting there, doodling on the pad. The phone rang a few times before it was picked up.

"What is it baby? Is everything alright?" I could hear the music and the echoes of the crowd in the background. Quickly silenced as Dad had either gone into his office or the cooler.

"Yeah, Daddy everything is fine. Are you busy at the moment?"

"I'm never too busy for one of my favorite girls."
I took a seat on the couch.

"I have a favor to ask."

"What's that?"

"Sam found a young girl at the bar the other night. She's alone and has nowhere to go. He fears for her safety, as do I. I want to apply for emergency custody."

"Wait, slow down. A girl? Custody? You are only twenty-one, that's a huge responsibility. Have you thought about this? What about school?"

"School won't go anywhere. She needs a home and I know the only way I'll rest is if she's with us. Safe."

"Sweetheart, there's a."

"Daddy I really believe this girl is in danger and I don't want to see anything happen to her." I interrupted, as tears choked me. Every emotion about Katie's situation came rushing out.

"Calm down, honey. It's going to be okay."

"Daddy, we have to help her, please." My voice cracked as I spoke quietly.

"Okay, tell me what you can about her. I'll reach out to my friend down at CPS and see what they can do for her."

"Her name is Katie; she's sixteen years old. She has no one, her entire family is gone. She's from the area but didn't specify where."

"What does she look like?"

"Blonde hair, blue eyes, maybe five, three."

"That might be a tough request princess, there are tons of kids in the system." I felt urgency building in my chest at his words. I knew it would be hard, but it couldn't be impossible.

"Someone tried to kill her, Daddy." The other end of the phone was silent.

"I understand, princess, I'll do what I can."

"Where is this girl now?"

"She's here with me at Sam's apartment."

"You said he found her at the bar?"

"Yes, but Daddy, don't be mad at him, he got her out of there as soon as he saw her and he didn't say anything because she was so terrified, he wanted to find out what was going on before he said anything."

"I understand."

"Please, don't tell him I called you about this. I want you to find out what you can before I get his hopes up, he's desperate to help her."

"Alright, darling, I won't say anything. I have to go. I love you." I heard the background noise pick up again as he had gone back into the bar.

"I love you too." The call ended and I felt a weight lift from my chest. I took a moment to catch my breath before I went back out into the kitchen. Glancing at my phone, the time was just a little after two.

Katie was holding her head up with one of her hands, sleeping. I walked up to her gently and touched her shoulder. She jolted awake, launching herself backwards out of the chair. Crashing onto the floor. Her chest heaving, breathing heavy.

Then the unmistakable wheezing erupted.

"Katie?" I gently sat her up, but the wheezing worsened. I rubbed her back, trying to calm her down.

"Take a deep breath for me." There was a guttural sound and like a snap it stopped all together. Katie's eyes became filled with fear as she looked at me desperately. She began to shake and darted her eyes in the direction of the living room.

"Inhaler?" She nodded and I got up running into the other room. I checked the coffee table but there was nothing there.

"It's not here," I cried. I heard the door creak open and ran into the hallway. Fear creeping in as I watched it slowly open. My heart jumped when I saw it was Sam. He looked at me the terror evident.

"What's wrong?" I glanced into the kitchen and saw that Katie was now laying back on the floor, her eyes closed.

"Katie!" I rushed in, ignoring Sam. As I reached her, I heard his heavy footsteps rushing down the hallway, where he joined me at her side. He knelt down, scooping her up he carried her into the living room. My chest tightened as her arm draped off to the side and her head slipped into the crook of his forearm. He placed her on the couch and gently nudged her.

"Katie?" Her lips had parted, in a quiet gasp.

Sam looked to me.

"Where's her inhaler?"

"I don't know I looked for it on the table, but it wasn't there." Sam got down on his knees and began to feel around under the couch.

"Got it." He sat back on his heels and shook the inhaler before opening it and putting it in her mouth. He pushed the plunger down and then pulled it back. She didn't move.

"Come on Katie," I begged. Sam gently shook her arm, trying to get a response from her. We waited, the anticipation building as the tension in the room appeared to thicken.

It came like a fresh breeze; she coughed and then inhaled an unsteady breath. Relief flooded me as she opened her eyes, and I heard Sam sigh heavily with relief next to me. I reached out and pushed some strands of blonde hair out of her face. She blinked slowly, taking in another trembling breath, her head nodding ever so slightly.

"You're going to be okay. We got you." The words came out with uneasiness. She took another quiet gasp and then closed her eyes. I turned to Sam, who was rubbing his hand over his face.

"Should we take her to the hospital?" I asked.

"I don't know, that was a really bad one."

"She needs help." I looked back at Katie, and her eyes didn't reopen. I shook her gently. "Katie?" For a moment, my heart stopped believing the worse, when a soft hum came from her.

"That one took a lot out of her. Let her sleep," Sam said softly as he took my hand. I nodded and let him gently pull me to my feet. His arm snaked around my shoulders, hugging me tightly to him, before leading me out of the room. I could feel myself shaking against him as we walked.

Crossing the threshold into the kitchen, I fell apart. Sam turned me so that I was facing him. Burying my face into his shoulder I let it all out as he held me tightly to him.

"It's okay," he cooed quietly. His hand was smoothing my hair; every breath I took was filled with the faint smell of his cologne and the evident smell of alcohol and cigarette smoke from the bar.

"I can't even bring myself to imagine what would have happened if you hadn't come home when you did," I sobbed quietly, I felt my body tremble. He shushed me softly and continued to hold me until my tears stopped flowing.

CHAPTER
30

S am made a pot of coffee, and we sat up in the kitchen, checking on her often. I sat in the chair closest to the threshold, the table turned so that I could get up and rush into the living room if need be. After witnessing her panic attack and almost watching her suffocate, I couldn't shake the feeling of a sword hanging by a hair. Like at any moment, it was going to drop. I could feel the tension in my body as I silently and intently listened into the other room.

"If you want to go to bed, babe, you can. I can stay up with her." Sam's voice broke the silence and the wavelength between the rooms was broken.

"No, it's my fault. I should stay with her," I sighed as I leaned back in the chair.

"You didn't do anything. All you did was try to wake her up. You didn't cause this." He stood up from his chair and walked over, standing behind me.

"She could have died." My voice edgy as the words spilled out of my mouth. He put his hands on my arms and began to rub them.

"But she didn't. She's okay." I wrapped my arms around myself. The stiffness inside seemed to radiate out of me and his hands stopped on my shoulders, gripping them softly.

"What's wrong?" he asked.

"I had a nightmare?" I felt him shift behind me as he walked around and knelt beside me. My eyes met his and concern was rooted deep within his intense blue eyes.

"Was it him?" There was a snarl in his voice as he spoke. I watched his eyes change, from concern to subtle anger as I nodded my head.

"What did he do?" I looked over at the couch. I couldn't see Katie, but I knew she was on the other side. Tears began to fall, as her lifeless eyes popped into my mind.

"He killed Katie." I dropped my hands into my lap as the words came out, he took them in his, squeezing them gently.

"Why would she be in your dream?"

"I don't know. My Dad brought it up earlier when I was at the bar."

"You came to the bar?" Shit. I forgot that I hadn't talked to him while I was there.

"It was only for a minute; Daddy threw me out because it was getting rowdy."

"What did you come down to the bar for?" I didn't want to tell him what I had heard on the radio. Whatever that was, wasn't what was happening here. Katie couldn't be the same girl that the police were looking for.

"I forgot to buy soda at the market, so I wanted to grab a few cans from the bar." Sam seemed to relent, as though my response was good enough. My chest relaxed from its tense hold as he let go of my hands and sat back on his heels.

"You know how he feels about you being down there." I nodded and then changed the subject.

"Did you talk to your Dad?"

"Yeah." Sam stood up and rubbed the back of his neck with his hand.

"What did your Dad have to say?"

"Said he was just checking in."

"Does he do that a lot?"

"No, that's why it's odd."

It had been odd.

The way that I had felt finding him in the stair-well.

Sam had felt it during their encounter as well.

"I wonder why he came all this way. Did he say how long he was staying?"

"He said he was going to stay for a few days."

"Are you going to see him again?"

"Yeah, he wants to get dinner with us Monday."

"What about Katie?"

"I'll have to tell him about her."

"How do you think he will react?"

"I don't know. My Dad and I." He stopped. "We've never been close. He's been trying since the accident, but we are pretty stagnant." I reached out and took his hand.

"If it would be easier, I can stay home with her." Sam sighed as his eyes glanced towards the living room.

"Only if you want to. I don't feel like going alone. I might just cancel."

"You should spend some time with your Dad." I didn't want him to go, not after what had just happened, but he needed to figure things out. His Dad came all this way to see him.

"If you are comfortable with it. You seemed pretty startled by him." His eyes flashed into my mind, and I felt a shiver silently run down my spine.

"I'll stay to help with Katie. You need to work things out with your Dad and find out more about what happened to you." I reached out and took his hand. "You need closure." He leaned forward and planted a soft kiss on my lips, sending a buzz through my entire body.

"I don't know what I would do without you." I reached up and gently cupped his cheek with my hand.

"I try my best," I replied with a slight smile.

When I woke up, I realized that I was in bed but didn't remember making the journey to it. Rolling over, I reached for Sam. Gripping the soft flannel sheets where he usually slept, I sat up when I realized he wasn't there. My eyes drifted to the nightstand, where my phone was charging. Picking it up, the bold letters on the screen read a quarter after eight. As the blankets fell, exposing my bare shoulders to the air a chill ran down my spine. I unplugged my phone and got up. Pulling my cardigan from behind the door, I wrapped it around me, letting it's warmth embrace me quickly.

Quietly, I made my way down the hallway. As I entered the living room, I found Sam sleeping in the chair, as Katie slept soundly on the couch. I slowly backed out and crossed the hall into the kitchen.

Dumping the left-over coffee from last night, I started a fresh pot. Looking out the window overlooking the back alley, where our cars were parked, I could see fresh snow had fallen in the night. The window was slowly stretching an icy shade over itself. Crossing the small room, I stared at the thermostat, it was set to sixty-seven, but the room was reading forty-four. I tapped it a few times and switched it on and off. Waiting patiently, I heard the thunderous rumble of the furnace as it kicked to life and warm air drifted softly over my bare feet. I was welcoming the warmth when Sam startled me. His hair was sticking up, his eyes were red with sleepiness, and he was still in his clothes from his shift.

"Did I wake you?" I asked. I walked up to him and gently placed my hands on his chest. I felt his chest rise as he took in a breath.

"No," he yawned. His hands resting on my hips.

"When did I go to bed?"

"I carried you in about four-thirty." I stood on my tip toes and kissed him softly.

"I'm sorry. I told you that I would stay up with you."

"That's alright."

"How's Katie?" Sam gently pulled his hands from me and rubbed the back of his neck as he turned to look back into the living room.

"She had a rough night."

"Really? What happened?" My eyes darted to the living room, although my feet remained planted.

"She woke up a few times, needed the inhaler at least once." I looked at him and then back towards the living room. I sighed heavily and turned my eyes back to Sam.

"Has she told you what she sees?" Sam shook his head no.

"I don't have the heart to ask her," he confessed. I crossed the kitchen again and looked in the living room as I heard a shuffle on the couch.

"She's been through hell," I said, my voice trailing off slightly as a single tear slid down my face. Sam walked over, turning me towards him, quickly wiping it away.

"She has. The important thing is she is safe now." I nodded and blinked forcing away the other tears that threatened.

"What's the plan for the day?" I asked with a forced smile, distracting myself from the feelings welling in my chest. He sighed heavily and leaned his head back.

"I promised your Dad, I would do inventory. I have to go in here shortly."

"Do you think she would like to go shopping or something?" His eyes met mine again and they were shining.

"You could ask her. It wouldn't hurt for her to get out of the apartment for a bit." I nodded.

"We can have a little girl's day." Sam kissed my forehead.

"I have a little money saved up, I'll put it on the nightstand in case she finds something she likes." I nodded and he turned me around, pressing his chest to my back and holding me tightly against him.

"Sam?"

"Hmh," he hummed against the dip between my neck and my collarbone.

"Thank you for letting me help." I felt his lips grace my neck softly, my breath hitching in my throat.

"Thank you for being open minded and helping me with her." His words cast warmth on my neck as he spoke. I leaned my head back on his shoulder.

"I love you." The silence that followed was deafening; we had only been seeing each other for four months. My head turned up to look at him, and he was staring down at me. Slowly, he leaned down and kissed me gently.

"I love you, too." Shuffling grabbed both of our attention, and we parted. Katie stood in the entryway, rubbing her eyes.

"Good morning," Sam said. She nodded with a yawn.

"Would you like to get out for a little bit?" Sam asked. She looked at him curiously. "I have to work this morning, but Scarlett has offered to take you shopping." Her eyes moved to me, and I smiled.

"Girls day." At first she seemed unsure, but quickly a small smile spread across her face.

"I have some clothes I brought over for you. You don't want to go in those grumpy old man clothes," I teased.

"Old man?" Sam chuckled, putting his hand over his heart like he was wounded. The scar on his arm flashed from under his sleeve. Another reminder of his accident. My eyes traced back to Katie, and she stood wide eyed.

"Katie, what's wrong?" She blinked and I saw tears welling in her eyes. I moved towards her and pulled her into a hug. Smoothing her hair as I cooed quietly. She reminded me of my own sister; they were close in age.

When I pulled away I put my hands on her shoulders and smiled. Her eyes were still on Sam, as he stood completely oblivious.

"Let's go have some fun," I chirped. Her eyes met mine, once dim, now brightened by the invitation, despite the lingering tears. She nodded before walking off to the bathroom.

When she emerged, her hair was still wet from her shower, wearing one of the outfits I had thrown together. Strands of her long blonde hair plastered her neck, almost highlighting the bruises. Her eyes lowered as she reached up, she noticed.

"You look nice," I said. She nodded her head as though she was thanking me but refused to look up. I gently took the hand that lingered at her side. Her eyes lifted, meeting mine.

"I have something for that." Her eyebrows shifted quizzically. I led her down the hall to Sam's room. Walking in, she remained in the doorway. Rummaging through the box of clothes, I quickly found what I was looking for. A plum knitted scarf. It would be perfect with the beige cardigan she wore. I turned, exiting the room and draped it around her neck, wrapping it as a double, covering the bruises. It was thin, so it wouldn't be too bulky or uncomfortable. I stood back admiring it.

"What do you think?" She padded into the bathroom. Standing in the doorway I watched her examine the scarf. She put her hands through her hair trying to get the remaining strands out from underneath. She turned her body towards me and as she raised her arms, the shirt she wore underneath rose ever so slightly. My eyes caught a glimpse of a rigid, circular scar, about two inches in diameter. It was darkened as though it was freshly healed. My breath hitched and she looked at me. Her eyes widened and she quickly turned away. I walked in gently, opening a drawer and grabbing a hairbrush. Acting as though I hadn't noticed.

"There's a hair tie on the handle if you want." She wouldn't look at me, the flash of embarrassment on her face was evident, as her cheeks crimsoned. I quietly walked out to leave her be.

Walking into the kitchen, Sam was filling his travel mug with fresh coffee. I leaned against the counter next to him and wrapped my arms around myself. He looked at me as he put the pot back on the warmer.

"What's wrong?" I felt my breath hitch as I opened my mouth to speak. My hand trailing over the scar that lingered, feeling the raised skin under the sleeve of my cardigan. A cold chill embraced me despite the warmth in the apartment.

"She has a scar." I paused. "Like from a bullet." My voice shook as the words flew out, quietly. His eyes widened.

"What?" His voice was low and panicked. He looked passed me and tried to take a step forward, but I put my hands on his chest, stopping him. He gently took my hands and looked deep into my eyes. I could feel the pressure behind my eyes as tears began to form.

"She was doing her hair, and I saw it, she has a gunshot scar on her left side." Sam looked out towards the hall and then back at me.

"Did it look recent?"

"It's healed, but it was dark, kind of like." My voice trailed off as my gaze drifted to my own arm, where I could clearly see in my mind's eye the ugly scar that remained from that night. I felt his fingers gently take my chin and turning my head up, my eyes flicked to his. Sadness dwelled deep within them.

"I will never, ever let anything like that happen again. To you or Katie." I nodded slowly as a single tear shed itself, rolling down my cheek. He pushed it away with his thumb and I cleared my throat standing straight. Today was going to be a good day, we were going to go shopping and get some lunch. I took a few deep breaths, centering myself, before nodding with confidence at Sam.

"You girls have fun today." He reached over to the counter, picking his travel mug up and securing the lid before kissing my cheek.

"See you after," I said, with a quiet smile. As he walked out into the hallway there was a brief silence.

"You look nice." I walked out. Katie had put her hair into a long, thick side braid. Sam looked back to me and smiled. "You did a good job, babe." I smiled and waved him off. He turned back to Katie.

"See you later." She nodded and he tousled her hair a little bit as he walked by. She playfully swung her arm at him. He turned with a smile and put his hands up, one wielding his coffee cup.

"Grass or gravel kid, you pick." Katie stilled almost immediately. Sam put his hands down, confusion lurking in his eyes. I stepped toward them and Katie turned into me, hugging me tightly.

"I didn't mean to scare her." His voice sad. She ferociously shook her head against me.

"I don't think it's that." I looked at him and silently mouthed the word 'brother.' He nodded and sighed heavily.

"I'll see you girls later."

"Have a good day." He nodded, then disappeared out the door. I rubbed Katie's arms as I gently pulled away from her.

"Come on, we have some shopping to do." I wiped away her tears, and she raised her sleeved hand to dry her face.

CHAPTER 31

We walked down towards Fifth and Broadway. There were plenty of people out shopping with it being Sunday. Katie stayed close to me as we walked, and I was telling her about all the local hot spots as we passed them by. She was young yet, but Nashville was a place of opportunity and the home of country music. Sure, there was a lot of bars and people filled the street every weekend with the intentions of celebrating or being discovered, but aside from that there was so much more the city had to offer.

"Do you like country music?" I asked. She nodded her head. I pulled the small notepad and the pen I had purchased from my coat pocket and handed it to her. "Who's your favorite country artist?" She scribbled.

"Carrie Underwood."

"I love her, her Storyteller album has got to be one of my favorites."

"Me too." She wrote.

"Favorite color?"

"Blue."

"Pineapple on pizza."

"Absolutely."

"Favorite movie?"

"The Labyrinth." The movie played in my mind's eye from last night.

"I didn't realize it was an older movie. I really enjoyed it. Who introduced you to that?"

"My mom." Her gaze shifted as we walked.

"How long has it been?" I asked quietly. She picked up the pad and scratched against it.

"Almost two years."

"I'm sorry." She nodded.

"What about your Dad?"

"Not long after mom."

"And your brother." She put the pen to the paper, stopping as she released a heavy and sad sigh, clearing her throat.

"Eight months."

"What happened to him? If you don't mind me asking."

"Drowned." My heart shattered into a million pieces when I read it. She had lost everyone that made her world go round and now she was running, escaping someone who was a shadow to anyone else, but deadly to her. I stopped, taking her hands in mine.

"Katie, do you like staying with us?" She nodded.

"Would you be okay with staying.with us permanently?" Her eyes grew wide, and her eyebrows raised in question. "Sam and I would really like for you to stay with us." She seemed taken aback by what I had just said, but shortly her eyes crinkled as she smiled and shook her head yes. I stood back up and pulled her into a hug. Sam hadn't exactly voiced to me his desire for her to stay, but the way he was with her, he seemed to open up. Like having her around helped bring out part of who he was before the accident.

He seemed happier.

Now I just had to wait on Daddy to get back to me about what his people were able to do.

We walked around the shops and looked at everything. Katie ended up purchasing some small items, like a black hoodie from Ariat and a pair of sweatpants from Nike. Sam had left out a thousand dollars for her to spend if she wished, but she only wanted those things. I looked down at her shoes. It was cold this time of year and her shoes although weren't in bad shape, were not meant for this type of weather. I could see that they were wet from our walk and could only imagine that her feet were freezing.

"Let's get you some boots, those shoes are going to make you sick." She looked down at her shoes and then up at me. She nodded slightly and I led her towards Carhartt.

As we went inside we quickly found the boots, looking through them, she tried on several pairs before deciding on a black pair of Pellston's.

"Do you like them?" I asked. She nodded.

"Well let's get them then." She took the boot off and returned it to the box, her eyes widening as she saw the price tag. She looked at me and pointed it.

"Don't worry about it," I said. She looked at me as though she was questioning if I was sure. I put my hand on her shoulder.

"It's something you need. Don't worry about the price, we are going to take care of you." She nodded slightly and closed the box. I took it from her and headed to the counter.

After leaving Carhartt, I heard a rumbling coming from Katie. I looked over at her, and she put her hands on her stomach and looked at me as though she was embarrassed. I pulled my phone from my back pocket; we had been there for a little while and it was about lunchtime.

"Come on," I said as I nodded my head in the direction of the food hall.

As we walked into the food court, she stood astounded by the number of choices.

"What are you in the mood for?" My stomach was grumbling as we hadn't eaten breakfast before we left. She walked ahead a little bit, and I followed close behind. She seemed to be studying the restaurants carefully, trying to decide.

She stopped just outside of a stall and looked back at me questioningly. I looked up at the sign.

"Cheese Lab?" I asked. She nodded her head. "Sounds good to me."

As we sat a table with our grilled cheese, I asked more questions, and she jotted them down on the paper.

"What grade are you in?"

"Sophomore."

"How are your grades?"

"Decent."

"Where do you go? Brentwood? Eastside? Glen-cliff?"

"Home schooled."

"That's got to be tough."

"I used to go to regular school, until recently." It felt as though my food had become stuck in my throat as I swallowed, as I read what she had written. My mind floated back to the bruises on her neck. Was that why she was pulled from school? To hide the abuse? Anger began to boil inside of me, and it seemed as though I had checked out of the present. A gentle hand on my arm brought me back quickly. Katie's hand pointed to the pad of paper on the table. I looked down reading it.

"Can we head back?" I looked at the time on my phone. We had been out for a least two hours.

"Yeah, we can head back. Sam's probably almost done anyway. He should be off the rest of the night, so we can all do something." She nodded with a smile, and we finished eating.

As we walked into the bar, almost immediately, Sam came rushing out of the back, grabbing me by my arm, and pulling me behind him. Standing between me and Katie like a shield.

"Who are you?" His voice was raised and directed at Katie. She dropped her shopping bags, the contents spilling out onto the floor.

"Babe, what are you doing?" I asked as I tried to go around him. He firmly put his arm out barring me. His body lurched forward, and I heard plastic hit the floor, like a slap.

"Tell me!" Katie shuddered at his harshness, tears forming in her eyes. I felt the urge to rush around him and take her in my arms. I grabbed his arm to move it.

"GET OUT!" Sam yelled. Katie stumbled as she backed into the door, pulling it open and running out.

"Sam what the hell?" I asked, my voice raised ever so slightly. He bent down and when he stood he handed me a Virginia license. My eyes widened as I read the name. Katie was the girl from the radio.

"It's her," I said, disbelief filled me at the realization. I looked from the ID back to the door. I had to go after her.

"What do you mean?"

"That's Isabel, the girl from Virginia. She's in danger."

"What are you talking about?" He was still coming down from his outburst, his voice still heated.

"She's missing from Virginia, she needs help."

"She lied to us."

"Sam, she's a scared girl. The Virginia police have been looking for her; she truly is in danger." I darted around him and out the door, hoping that she hadn't made it too far.

"Isabel!" I yelled as I ran down the street. I saw her sliding on the sidewalk as she turned the corner.

"Scarlett." I heard Sam calling me, but I had to catch up with her.

As I ran around the corner, my feet slid in the snow as I stopped, when I spotted the man. His back turned to me, Isabel visibly struggling in his arms, as he tried to force her towards a car that ran in the street nearby.

"Hey!" I yelled. He spun on me suddenly and fear gripped at my chest.

"Don't move," he said.

"What are you doing?" I put my hands up as the hooded man had his hand over Isabel's mouth, holding her tightly to him as the barrel of his gun was trained on me. She struggled against him, tears streaming down her face as small, muffled cries, emanated from behind his hand.

"She's coming with me."

"You're hurting her." It came out calmly, despite the pounding in my chest. I took a small step forward and he shook his gun at me.

"Now, Scarlett, don't make me shoot you and leave you to die in the street." I stopped.

"It was, you." The realization slapped me in the face.

"It was, yes." Shock riddled my body, like being struck by lightning.

"Why are you here now? What do you have to do with Isabel?"

"Reasons that have nothing to do with you." I looked at Isabel as she struggled beneath his hold. His hand gripping so tightly to her face, I could see she was struggling to breathe. If he didn't let go, she could go into a panic attack, and I didn't have her inhaler with me.

"Let her go." The shudder evident as the words came out.

"I'm afraid I won't be doing that."

"What do you want with her?"

"That is none of your concern." I took another step forward and this time he shifted the gun of the barrel, pressing it to Isabel's head. I froze where I stood as a high-pitched squeal came from her. She stopped fighting and shook violently under the pressure of the barrel. My heart broke as I looked into her red-rimmed teary eyes, begging me silently for help. My mind was running rampant, I had to help her, but I didn't know how, not with him ready to pull the trigger given any reason to.

"Don't!" I put my hand up in front of me, as though trying to reach out to him, trying to get him to train the gun on me again. My voice cracked under the weight of the pressure and tears formed in my eyes.

"Walk away." I took another step toward him, and he pushed the gun harder against her head. "NOW!" His voice was guttural.

"Please, don't do this, she's just a little girl," I begged. He laughed callously as he pulled back on Isabel, making her cry out again.

"You think pleading with me will help? You have no idea who you are dealing with. Now, I'm giving you one last chance. Walk. Away." My eyes were trained on Isabel, but then my eyes darted back to him.

"I'll scream, there are plenty of people nearby, you won't get away."

"Go ahead. You'll both be dead before someone reaches the corner." His voice was sinister, I didn't dare move, he began to walk backwards towards the car, dragging Isabel with him. She threw her weight around, forcing him to drop the gun and she sprinted forward from his arms towards me. He retrieved the gun from the ground quickly. I reached my hand out for her as he pointed the gun. Ready to drag her in my arms and get between them. We had both been through this before, but I was not about to let her die in the street.

My mind glimpsed to Sam; he would never forgive me. A shot rang out, deafening us. I felt her fingers in my hand grazing it, before she was ripped away from me, her hand slipping away from mine before I even had a chance to grasp it.

"No!" I yelled. I took two steps forward and fell to my knees as a searing pain ripped through my right leg. I put my hand over where the pain came from and looking down at my fingers, blood smeared across them.

He pulled her back towards the car on the curb.

Hitting her over the head, her body hit the ground with a sickening thud, making my heart quake. I forced myself to my feet and took another painful step forward as he stood by the open door, Isabel now in the backseat.

"Let her go!" I growled loudly. He turned his gun back to me.

"Don't make me shoot you again, Scarlett."

"You'll have to kill me before I let you take her." He slammed the door shut, sending me into a rage.

I wasn't going to let him do this.

I ran forward, fighting the pain that shot through my body, a familiar friend that I had acquainted once before. A smirk appeared in the corner of his mouth as he raised his face slightly towards the light.

Those eyes!

Another shot rang out, shattering the quiet with a fierce echo.

CHAPTER
32

I held my hand tightly over my leg as I stumbled up to the door of the bar. Turning the knob, I opened it and stumbled in.

As the door closed behind me, Dad appeared from the back. His smile weakened at the sight of me. He rushed to me, taking me in his arms.

"Scarlett, what happened?" I winced as the pain shook me.

"Where's Sam?"

"He's in the back."

"Can you get him?" I groaned as I fought the desire to fall to the floor. Dad's eyes widened.

"You're bleeding." His attention immediately went to my leg, which was now soaked in blood. "We need to get you to the hospital."

"No time." I went down on my knees, despite the fight, a groan of pain escaping me. Dad grabbed a towel from the counter and rushed over.

"Sit back, baby." I rolled over so that I was sitting down, and he tied the towel above the wound, the pressure from him tightening it made me cry out. "That son of a bitch." He cursed under his breath.

"What?" He looked at me and there was something in his eyes. Something he was now fighting deep within. A resemblance of regret.

"Nothing." He tore his eyes away from me and looked down, inspecting my leg.

"Daddy, tell me." He continued staring at my leg, like he couldn't hear me. "Isabel's life is in danger."

"Stay out of it."

"No! Tell me what you know." Nothing was making sense. Who had taken her? Why? How was my dad involved? He looked at me and shook his head, focusing on the wound trying to determine if it was fatal or not.

"It's a flesh wound, just a graze," he said quietly. He looked back up at me. "You're going to be just fine."

"Daddy, tell me that you didn't make a deal with that man." His eyes locked with mine and the answer lied within. My heart felt as though it was being ripped to shreds. "Why?"

"He threatened you and your sister; I couldn't take that risk."

"Why did he take her?"

"I don't know."

"What does he want with her?"

"That's none of our concern."

"How did he find her?" Again, his eyes gave him away. My eyes widened. "Daddy, please tell me you didn't call him."

"When he was here a few months ago, he returned after and gave me this picture." He fished his wallet out and pulled a folded picture out of his billfold. He opened it and showed it to me. It was a school photo of Isabel.

"Why?"

"He said he was looking for her and that if she ever came here, he wanted me to call him. I told him to get the hell out at first and then he brought up you and Taylor." He stopped talking and took a staggered breath. "You know I would do anything to protect you girls."

"How did you even know for sure it was her?"

"I checked the security cameras."

"So, that's it, a deranged man is looking for a young girl, and you thought it was a good idea to go along with it?" My voice was raised, not only from the pain leeching from my leg, but also from the anger I felt in my heart.

"He is an immensely powerful man, with powerful friends. He asked me to call him if she ever came here and let him know. I did tell him no, but then he said he would kill you and Taylor."

"He's already shot me twice now. If he threatened to kill me and Taylor, what do you think he is going to do with Isabel?"

"I don't know." I felt anger rising in my chest.

"Dad, he took her at gunpoint," I cried. He was silent. "Did you know all of this when I called you asking for help?" There were tears welling in his eyes.

"Yes."

"Did he know?"

"Yes."

"How long has he known?"

"I saw her on the camera, before she found Sam. I called him the moment she walked in. I had no idea she was going to go to Sam. I was just going to let her walk out the door and tell him she had been here but had left and I had no idea where she was. I never expected you or Sam to get attached to her and let her stay upstairs."

"What are we going to do?"

"Nothing. It's out of our hands," he sighed.

"This is on our hands." A painful groan escaped me once more as the pain flashed hotly in my leg. The makeshift tourniquet making my leg throb as it cut off the blood supply.

"Let me take you to the hospital."

"No. We need to stop him." I tried to push myself up, but his hands were on my arms keeping me on the floor.

"You'll bleed out."

"You said it was just a graze."

"That doesn't mean you won't bleed to death." I didn't care; I wanted to find him and get Isabel back. The more time we spent wasting here, the further they got away.

"We need to save her."

"There's nothing we can do."

"Sam needs to know."

"Can't you just let it go?" He spat with frustration.

"No. We promised her she would be safe." He looked into my eyes, and I found myself pleading with him. This man was one of the kindest people I had ever known, who would do anything for his family. My heart broke thinking about how he felt he had no other way; he was going to let her go. I knew he would do anything to protect my sister and me, but even if he let her go, how much time would that have given him? What was his plan past that? "She's a child who needed to be protected, and you sold her out to the devil." My words were laced with venom. Everything began to get blurry, darkening as I began to lose consciousness.

"Sam!" Dad yelled. Sam came in from the back, dropping the clipboard in his hand, it made a clacking sound as it hit the tiles. The darkness began to take over, and he became a shadow. His arms wrapped around me pulling me tightly to him.

"Call nine one-one."

When I woke up, I was sitting up in a bed at the hospital. I looked down at my leg and saw there was a gauze patch on it, there was a little bit of blood seeping through the gauze, leading me to believe that they hadn't stitched it yet. The door opened and I looked up to see the friendly face of a nurse.

"How are you feeling?" she asked.

"Terrible."

"Can't say I'm surprised."

"What's going to happen now?" I asked softly.

"Well, the doctor is going to come in and stitch you up, your x-ray just came back, and it looks like there are no bullet fragments remaining." Her words jolted my memory.

"Sam?"

"I beg your pardon?"

"My boyfriend, Sam. Is he here?"

"I can check."

"I need to speak with him immediately."

"Alright, I'll see if I can find him." She walked out shutting the door behind her. I raised my hands and held them over the top of my head as I anxiously waited, everything replaying in my mind.

His eyes flashed.

I knew who he was.

But I had no proof.

When I heard the door open, I sat up straight in bed, my eyes on the door as he walked in.

"Babe?" His voice cracked as he spoke. My eyes filled with tears at the sight of him. The eyes I knew to be broody and the face that held so much strength, held nothing but rigid concern and distress.

"Baby, you have to find her," I sobbed. He rushed to my side, I pushed my head against his chest as he sat on the bed next to me, pulling me into his arms. I was sobbing uncontrollably, trying to catch my breath.

"What do you mean?"

"Isabel."

"What happened, baby?" I pulled away from him, and he cupped my face in his hands. He swiped tears away with his thumbs and I took a shaky breath.

"He was there when I got there."

"Who?" His eyes went back and forth trying to read my face.

"He took her, and I tried to stop him, that's when he shot me." I saw his chest heave as I said the words. His concern was quickly replaced with anger.

"Who did this? Who took her?" He asked urgently. My breath hitched in my throat as I prepared to answer him, my heart breaking as the words flew from my mouth.

"The man who robbed the bar." I watched his eyes as they reacted, but his face remained the same. He didn't expect that to be the response he would get. He reached up brushing away my tears.

"It's going to be okay. I'm going to find her." I nodded.

"Go," I pleaded. He leaned in kissing me hard on the lips. He headed to the door, stopping as he opened it and turning to me.

"I love you." The crashing of the world around me stopped for a brief moment at his words.

"I love you, too."

"I'll be back."

"Babe, there's something you need to know." He closed the door slightly, turning his attention to me completely. I struggled with what I was about to tell him, but he needed to know how this happened. He needed to know everything. I would never keep anything from him, especially knowing what I knew now.

"What is it?"

"My Dad knew."

"What do you mean?"

"He called him. He saw her on the camera the night she came in."

"Why didn't he say anything?"

"He told Daddy he would kill Taylor and me, if he refused to help him." I breathed out heavily as I said the words out loud, making my chest ache at the thought.

Torment flashed in his eyes.

Chest heaving with an invisible anger.

I wanted to comfort him, but before I could say anything else, he turned once more toward door. Hand on the handle.

"There's something else."

He stopped.

Not turning to look at me.

Not right away.

"What?"

"His voice was familiar."

He turned then.

"What do you mean?"

I felt the tears in my eyes.

It was in that moment.

Realization hit him.

His eyes wide.

How could I tell him that it was his father I had seen?

PART FIVE

CHAPTER 33

"Who are you?" I felt my body tremble; his normally kind face was filled with anger and his words laced with poison. He threw something down and I glanced at it. The bags fell from my hands.

"Tell me!" I took a shaky breath as I looked down at my driver's license, tears welling in my eyes as my gaze snapped back up to meet his.

I wanted to explain.

But I couldn't.

"GET OUT!" I backed up, nearly tripping as I did so quickly, my back slammed against the door before I turned around, yanking it open and running down the street.

"Isabel!" I heard my name echo from behind me. As I turned the corner, turning my head slightly, looking back. I saw Scarlett running out after me, when I ran into something hard and hands roughly gripped my arms, turning me and pushing me towards an open car door. I kicked and tried to pull myself free, desperate whimpers escaping me as a hand flew around and slapped tightly over my mouth.

"Hey!" He spun, pulling a gun from his waistband in a fluid motion that could have made me sick.

My eyes shot towards the voice.

Scarlett.

She stopped in her tracks as I saw the barrel of the gun pointed at her.

"Don't move," he said.

"What are you doing?" Scarlett asked as she put her hands up. She took a few steps forward.

I felt the metal barrel against my head. Hot tears streamed ferociously down my face as I looked to Scarlett for help.

She stood.

Helpless.

His voice familiar.

He came from nowhere.

So fast, I didn't see his face.

He began to pull me back and I threw my weight against him, throwing off his balance. My feet pounded the pavement, racing toward Scarlett as I heard the gun clatter against the asphalt. She reached her hand out.

Our fingers touching.

Slipping.

A gunshot rang out behind me.

Nothing but air.

A crushing grip on my arm pulling me back.

Safety.

Scarlett.

Only steps away.

Now gone.

"No!" She cried. I watched her take a few steps and then fall to the ground. Her hand moved to her leg. Blood was seeping into the snow on the sidewalk. Pulling against the arm around me desperate to get to her.

Desperate to help her.

Instantly, everything went dark.

The echo of a gunshot following me into the void.

As my senses returned, my head throbbed. I could smell the leather from the backseat of the car as it soared smoothly down the road. The engine quiet. My body felt heavy as I laid there. Turning my head, my eyes found the rearview mirror, where his eyes met mine.

Weston.

"You really did it this time. It was supposed to be an easy job, take you and your little friends out and then that was it, but no, you had to make things difficult. You're like a bad habit; you just keep coming back up after being put down. Killing Soren Cross was the shot heard around the world." He sniffled as he spoke, the car speeding up. I pushed myself up slowly. Sitting there I glared at him through the mirror.

"Don't look at me like that. You did this to yourself." My heart was pounding in my chest; this man was supposed to be dead.

Anger filled me.

Why was this monster allowed to live when my brother wasn't?

I leaned forward and he moved quickly, pointing his gun at me over his shoulder. I slammed back against the seat, instinctively throwing my hands up in front of me.

"That's what I thought. You just keep sitting there and behave. We are almost there." I kept my eyes on him through the rearview mirror. Though the windshield revealed that the day had become night. I tried to recognize the area we were in, but there was nothing that led me to any memory. There were big metal warehouses around us, all of them were dark as no one seemed to be around.

When the car stopped, two men approached. Weston got out of the car and kept his gun on me as they opened the door to grab me out. I threw myself down on the backseat, trying to kick at them. One of them managed to grab my foot and pull me out of the car, dropping me onto the ground. He sat on top of me, and I was transported to that day.

To Soren.

I threw my hands out as desperate wails came from deep inside, fear rising into every nerve as I thrashed, trying to get him off. He grabbed my arms and threw them down against the ground, pinning me.

"She's a fighter this one." He spoke with a sickening chuckle that made my stomach churn.

"Get her inside," Weston ordered. My eyes flicked to him, and he put his gun away in its holster as he shut the car door. The other man walked over and together they got me up. Throwing me against the back of the car, forcing my hands behind my back, and tying them. With one on each side, they grabbed me under my elbows and walked me toward a warehouse.

As the door opened and they pushed me inside, the room was dark. Quickly a light came on, and I turned my head back, glancing over my shoulder, watching Weston follow behind.

A smile on his face.

Pleased.

Like an awaiting executioner with an axe behind his back.

They shoved me forward until we reached a chair, they turned me in front of it and then sat me back, lacing my arms around the back of the chair.

"Should we gag her?" One of them asked as he walked around the chair and stood before me.

"That won't be necessary." He knelt down in front of me, a twisted smile appearing at the corner of his lips. "This little birdie can't sing." He laughed as he mocked me and I began to pull on the chair, kicking my legs at him. He stood back, pulling a pack of cigarettes from his back pocket, he lit one.

"What are we going to do with her, boss?"

"I wanted to wait for Solomon, but the timeline just moved up." He stopped looking at me. A shudder ran through my body at his words. With everything that had happened, I had forgotten all about the trial and if I weren't there to testify, Solomon would walk free. A ringing echoed throughout the warehouse, coming from Weston's pocket. He pulled his phone out and answered it, putting it on speaker.

"Yes, sir?"

"Have you acquired the package?" His voice sent shivers down my spine, a cold touch of death lingering in every syllable he spoke.

"Right here."

"Did you have any trouble?"

"A little bit." My eyes widened.

Scarlett.

What had happened to her?

My mind rampantly ran through what I remembered. He grabbed me and he pointed his gun at her.

She tried to help, and he put the gun to my head.

Then he started pulling me backwards.

I felt her hand as a phantom drift over my bound hands.

She was bleeding.

Tears welled in my eyes as I remembered the blood stained snow. As hard as I tried to remember what came next.

I couldn't.

My pleading eyes found Weston's and in them I was begging to know the answer.

"How did you handle it?" Weston smiled as he anticipated the question and was even happier to respond.

"I put it down." Tears sprang from my eyes at his words. She was innocent and he had no reason to shoot her.

She just wanted to help me.

He only did it because he wanted to, the sick bastard. I shook my head violently, before my lungs began to cave on themselves, sending me into a full-on panic attack. The room seemed to shrink to the smallest size, and I felt like I couldn't breathe.

"What's wrong?" Solomon asked through the speaker.

"Nothing I can't handle." Weston walked briskly towards me and hit me across the face, dazing me. My head fell forward as I struggled to breathe, blood, trickling from my nose, trailing down my face over my lips. He grabbed my face roughly and forced my head up. My eyes lazily met his, a sinister stare in them, sending an icy chill to my very core.

"No, no. You don't get to go to sleep. You have to stay with us a little longer." Tears were still racing from my eyes as I thought about Scarlett.

"Don't cry. You'll see your friend again, very soon." He laughed and let go of my face, letting my head drop forward again.

"You'll pay for what you did." The voice snarled from the speaker on the phone. A quivering breath came from my nostrils, before breathing in the heavy scent of blood. I looked up.

"Fuck you." I mouthed as I spit blood onto the floor, just barely missing Weston's feet.

"Said fuck you, Sol," Weston said gleefully, as he stepped back from the blood on the floor. He stood straight, turning away as he continued his phone call. I squeezed my eyes shut as the horrific memories came flooding back. Seeing the faceless man's body falling to the floor. The dead man who had shot me in the woods as he entered my dreams so often. Jake before he disappeared into the ocean. Soren's sickly smile appeared behind my eyelids, and I rocked my body in the chair, trying to chase him away. I felt the legs of the chair teeter and then pain along my left side as the chair crashed to the floor.

"I suppose you'll be fine right there," Weston laughed. I opened my eyes, and everything was blurry. My head throbbed from bouncing off the concrete floor. If I were lucky, I was concussed, and sleep would release me from the binds of this rope; of this hellhole I was currently trapped in. Weston landed a swift kick to my body as he laughed. The blow sent the chair scraping against the floor, dragging me along with it. A guttural cough burst from my lips as I laid on the cold slab. I wanted to double over to wrap myself around the pain in hopes of relieving it but was unable.

"Sweet dreams."

My eyes fluttered and the lights went out.

"Isabel?" I opened my eyes at the sound of my name. I was looking out over the mountains, sitting on a rock face. The cool air gently blew around me, and the smell of the autumn leaves filled my senses. I turned my head and Jake sat next to me admiring the view.

"What are we doing here?"

"Living in the moment."

"What are you doing here?" He reached over and grabbed my hand, squeezing it gently.

"I told you; I would always be there for you."

"Am I dying?" The question came out quickly. He squeezed my hand again and looked at me, his eyes full of sorrow.

"I don't know." I rested my head on his shoulder, his cologne a soothing and familiar scent.

"I'd be okay with it."

"You would?"

"Yeah. I'm so tired of struggling to survive."

"It's too soon."

"It's not soon enough." He sighed heavily as he rested his head on top of mine.

"You're too young for this."

"We all are." I stopped myself. "Were."

"I never left you, you know." I felt tears quietly running down my face.

"I know."

"What do you think you will miss the most?"

"Dad." My voice quivered with my response. Dad was never going to overcome it. In two years,' time, he will have lost his entire family. One day, a man who had it all, a career, a loving wife and two adoring children, to suddenly having nothing left. My heart felt heavy thinking about him.

"You should stay with him."

"You should have stayed with him too."

"I had no choice."

"You did; you chose to." I stopped. It was pointless to argue with him; he was already dead.

"I chose to save you." More tears followed his words. "And given the chance I would do it again."

"But you can't save me this time."

He pulled away and whispered quietly into my ear.

"I'm still going to try."

"How? You aren't here." The words echoed out, and I immediately wanted to take them back. I looked into his eyes, as they exuded hurt at my words.

"I never left." His words echoed and then everything became dark as Jake, and the rock face disappeared.

CHAPTER
34

I opened my eyes, awoken by the shaking of my body as I laid on the freezing concrete floor. I slowly turned my eyes upwards towards the windows and could see a faint light dancing into the darkness. I let out a rattled breath. The chair shuddered and then I felt myself being lifted up off the floor.

"Sleep well?" Weston asked. I did actually, my only regret was that I had to wake up back in this shithole with these scumbags. In an instant, something came flying at me and I squeezed my eyes shut. As the freezing water drenched me, the moment flashed in my eyes.

Toppling from the boat.

The salty water searing my wounds.

Losing Jake.

Forever.

I opened my mouth gasping, spitting out the little bit that managed it's way in and my body shook.

"Thought you would like a little wake up call, you're looking a little tired." I glared at him, and he laughed, lighting up a cigarette.

"It's almost time for you to finally join your friend and family on the other side." He laughed sadistically. I pulled at the ropes that bound me, I was already going to die. I intended to go down fighting. Rage fueled me. The growing desire to knock that smirk off of his face, ever growing.

"Oh, feisty today aren't we?"

I responded with smugness.

He drew closer.

Too close.

"If it weren't for the fact that I was ordered not to, I would kill you and get it over with, but timing is everything." His voice was laced with hatred, inches away from my face.

He inhaled deeply as his eyes wildly searched mine for a reaction.

I stared at him dead pan.

I wouldn't give him the satisfaction of seeing my fear.

I didn't fear death.

Not anymore.

"Tell me Isabel, how have you been faring without dear Jakey boy?"

My brother's name on his lips enraged me.

My eyes slid across his face, shooting daggers.

"He held on tightly you know. In the end, desperate to keep me from reaching you." He eyed me up and down as I quaked under his dark eyes.

"And yet here we are. He failed." I pulled at my ropes, trying to reach him as tears of anger washed down my face.

"It's sad they never found him."

How would he know that?

How the hell did he even survive?

Questions, I knew I would never get answered.

Jake.

My idiot, protective brother.

He should have just let me go.

Weston's hand grabbed my chin tightly. My eyes meeting his.

"He died calling for you," he snickered.

My heart froze.

The question in my eyes.

Needing to know.

"The boat drug him down, where he died, slowly, painfully, as the air was crushed from his lungs by the pressure, your name being the last thing he cried."

I launched forward again.

"SHUT UP!" It came out strong. My eyes widening when I heard my own voice for the first time in months.

He cocked his head and smirked.

"So, this little birdie can sing."

"Want some more?" He was enjoying this game of his.

Our eyes met.

"Not very tough are you?" I spat in his face. He closed his eyes and wiped it away with a grimace. His mouth contorted in anger, eyes wild as he pulled back his foot and landed a kick to my stomach, sending the chair careening to the floor. A pained groan escaping me as the ropes bit at my skin.

One of the men approached, reaching for the chair.

"Don't," Weston ordered. The man retreated as Weston slicked back his black hair and pulled a pack of cigarettes from his pocket. Lighting one he shook his head. He blew smoke out and pointed his cigarette at me.

"See what happens when you try to be tough?" A smile crept into the corner of his lips.

"Boss?" Weston held up his hand, instantly silencing his man.

"She's not going anywhere. Leave her here." Weston walked around, keeping his eyes on me. He laughed and then began walking away as the other two followed.

As the door slammed shut behind them and the lock engaged, I laid there on the cold ground, my chest heaving.

Anger subsiding.

I didn't dare move.

Darkness in its shadowy form began to close in. I felt my chest rattle as I took a deep breath, remnants of my voice in the air lingered before everything went black.

I was bobbing up and down. Opening my eyes I was overlooking the open ocean, the water was turquoise blue, I could feel the warmth on my face as the sun brightly lit up around me. I turned my head to see Jake sitting next to me. We were sitting on the bow of a boat. His arms were resting on his knees as they were pulled tightly against him. His head buried in his arms.

"Jake?" His eyes met mine, the sadness evident with the tears that had trailed down his face.

"What?" I sighed softly. Feeling a few loose strands of hair, drifting around my face, I slowly swiped them away, delicately pushing them behind my ear. Something in my hair made my fingers tacky.

Dark red smeared across my fingertips.

I dropped my hand in my lap and looked at Jake. He sniffled as he grabbed my hand and turned it over, examining the blood on it.

I didn't even remember bleeding.

"You shouldn't have done that." I didn't regret my decision, not even a little bit.

"I'm going out on my own terms," I said soft-ly, gently taking my hand back from his grasp. I turned my gaze back out to the ocean.

"You should have waited," he sighed heavily.

"I've waited a long time." Tears sprung to my eyes as I looked at him, his eyes meeting mine. He reached his arm out, sliding his hand across my shoulders, pulling me tightly to him. I rested my head on his shoulder and my chest heaved heavily as peace radiated within. Soon, we wouldn't have to say goodbye anymore.

"It can't end this way. You're supposed to live," he sighed with a sniffle. He rested his head against mine.

"So were you." The silence that rendered be-tween us was like the sharp edge of a knife. Even the water was still.

"Isabel."

"I'm tired of fighting, Jake. I'm going to die any-way, whether it's today, tomorrow or one hundred years from now. My life will have just been a tiny blip on a massive timeline."

He pulled away from me.

Standing up he held his hand out to me, and I took it, he gently pulled me to my feet.

"You have people here that need you," he said as he held me at arm's length. I felt tears running down my face. The sky darkened and the boat began to rock tumultuously. I stumbled and he steadied me, my eyes meeting his.

"So did you." Lightning lit up the sky above us, the waves knocking against the boat. He pulled me into another hug, sniffling, as he kissed the top of my head hard. I wrapped my arms around him not wanting to let go.

"You need to wake up."

"No."

"WAKE UP!" He yelled over the roar of the thunder.

"I don't want to." It came out as a sob as I pushed my face against him.

"I'll see you soon." His voice was close to my ear. He pushed me back, holding me at arm's length, I opened my eyes, just as a giant wave began to tip the boat. My feet left the deck as he picked me up, pinning my arms tightly to my sides with his grip as he tossed me over the side.

"Jake!" I crashed into the water as the wave swallowed the boat and Jake whole.

CHAPTER
35

My eyes sprang open, and I was met with a grisly sight. The glazed over eyes, staring, the pungent smell of death profusely wrapping itself around me like a blanket, as I stared into the face that was once Soren Cross.

My arms had been freed, and the chair had been removed.

In my haste to move myself away from the body, my body revolted at the pain in my abdomen.

Pushing past it as best as I could, I got myself sitting up and pushed myself away from the corpse. The mouth hung open at a twisted angle, his eyes wide, the bullet wound in his forehead gaping. I turned my face away and squeezed my eyes shut but still saw him, not as a corpse but on top of me that day.

I couldn't escape him.

A hand forcefully grabbed my face and forced my head back in the direction of the body.

"Look at him! See what you've done!" I kept my eyes shut. Weston's voice, radiated hatred for me in my ear.

"I thought you would like the company." His sinister voice echoed across the room, bouncing off the walls. Silently I cursed my body for not letting me die while I was sleeping. It would have been better to die that way, then whatever way he intended for me. Still holding my face, Weston forced my face towards Soren's body again.

"You killed his brother, Isabel. Look at him. Look at what you did." I tried to pull my face free of Weston's grasp but didn't have the strength.

I turned my eyes to the dead body on the floor.

I felt my lips twist into a chaotic smile.

I wasn't sorry.

Not for what I did to him.

Because he would never be sorry for what he did to me.

"What are you smiling at?" Weston gripped my face tighter, as though he was going to break my jaw. He began to pull me from the ground by my face. He grabbed the back of my jacket to yank me up, my feet dangling in the air, gravity pulling my body down, pain rippling through, forcing me to scream out into the empty room.

"You have blood on your hands. How do you plead?" My eyes locked with Weston's.

They were wild

Fueled by chaos.

Thriving on entertainment.

I would never apologize for what I did. Letting him live would have been a disservice. Weston laughed as he dropped me back on the floor, another scream echoing from me.

"We are going to go on a little trip, but for now, I think you owe Soren an apology." He had dropped me right next to him, my head resting on the floor staring into those dead eyes. I couldn't move as the pain had stripped my body bare of any strength it may have held.

I was ready to be done.

I looked up at him as he walked away, leaving me there with Soren. His face horrific, burned into my memory for the rest of my life.

Hopefully, it won't be that much longer.

I closed my eyes, willing death to take me.

When I opened them again, Soren's dead eyes were staring at me. Even after what I had done, I couldn't bring myself to feel bad for him. Even now, with his body draped on the floor next to me. I wondered how they had gotten his body here and even more disturbingly, why they had brought his body in the first place. Solomon surely wouldn't have had let someone take his dead brother's body and parade it around just to prove a point.

Then again the man was without a doubt insane.

My eyes lifted from Soren's body as I heard the door across the building open. Two figures shrouded in the shadows entered, their faces becoming clearer as they approached.

"Looks like our little bird, is awake," Weston sneered. His hands were on me immediately, pulling me up from the ground. I was tired and just let Weston hold me up.

Dead weight.

My eyes locked with his and there was a flicker of something in them that I didn't quite grasp before he turned his head, breaking eye contact. There was something going on in his brain and I didn't know if I wanted to find out.

"I think you're guilty," Weston sneered into my ear. I turned my head towards Soren's body as it remained just at our feet and spat at it. Weston grabbed my face hard and forced it towards him, his dark eyes locking with mine once more, sending my stomach into tight knots.

"You really should show some respect for the dead." How ironic, he's the one who had the body brought here instead of letting him rest in hell where he belonged. If I could have told him to go to hell in that moment I would have, but my teeth where clenched shut under his forceful hold.

"Take a few swings boss, you need to let off some steam and decompress, you had a rough night," the other man sneered.

Weston let go of me and took a step back, leaving me barely standing there as my body swayed, lighting a cigarette. Hitting it, he blew the smoke in my face. As the smoke hit me I coughed.

He stood back and his sadistic smile returned.

Hitting it once more, his arm shot out, grabbing mine. Pulling it towards him, he dug the red-hot embers of his cigarette into my skin. My mouth opened as an audible scream, escaped into the room, bouncing off the walls.

He blew the smoke into my face, and I began coughing as he allowed me to rip my arm free of his grasp, clutching it. The burned flesh, black and red like a festering wound.

He cracked his knuckles.

The tell-tale sign that this was about to get ugly.

He was slow.

Deliberate

As he back handed me across the face, sending me to the floor.

My lip splitting from the contact.

He stepped back straightening himself.

Fixing his hair.

Taking a breath.

Collecting himself.

To anyone else it would appear to be over.

But I knew better.

He stalked toward me.

Grabbing the collar of my jacket, he hauled me up.

"You have a debt to pay," he said through gritted teeth. I came back and tightened my grip on his wrist, with what strength I had in me.

My eyes locked with his.

Fear flashed in his eyes.

Brief.

But real.

He knew what I had done.

By now he could see that I was content.

With the blood on my hands.

My impending doom.

He blinked.

Cold eyes returning.

"Go. To. Hell." My ears rang as the hoarse words sprang from my lips. A smile cracked between his lips.

"I'll see you there," he whispered.

He let go and I landed hard on the floor.

Darkness was quick to follow.

When I opened my eyes again, Soren was gone, and I was no longer on the concrete floor. Instead, I was in the back seat of the car, the familiar smell of the leather seat, fighting the lingering smell of death, the stark reminder of the lifeless body that had been left lying next to me on the floor. Lifting my gaze upwards, I saw Weston in the driver's seat. Outside the windows it had grown dark. A cough ripped from me, making me dizzy.

"It's just you and me now." His voice was laced with a sickening mixture of pleasure and danger. I ignored him, I had spent way too much time being afraid of him and whatever was going to come next was going to be my release from this hell. I took a shaky breath and felt a rattling in my chest. It wouldn't be long now and that wouldn't matter, the pain would go away, and I would reunite with Scarlett, Jake, and my mom.

The car continued smoothly down the road, until I felt the tires hit gravel, the crunch coming from under the car's weight as we continued driving was unmistakable. I couldn't help but wonder what he had planned for me, but I knew it wasn't going to be something simple. Solomon was a smart man, a man who did this for a living, he was going to have Weston make an example of me, to keep anyone else from thinking twice about doing what I had done. The thought knocked at my chest. I had taken away someone that Solomon loved. It was a wild thought to me, that Solomon was capable of loving anyone, especially since the man was a complete fucking psycho.

My mind began to wonder if he had a wife or children. I quickly pushed it away, if he had children, then he wouldn't be able to do this easily.

Not hunt down and murder children.

What father would do that to someone else's kids?

But Soren was his little brother and if there was one thing I was certain of as I experienced it myself, is that an older sibling would do anything to protect their younger ones. My mind brought forth those last moments with Jake. How he had held Weston back from reaching me before the boat overturned.

Before I lost him.

My whole life he had always protected me.

My mind flickered back to the dream.

"I'll see you soon." His words echoed.

Even in death, he was still trying to save me.

The sound of the car scraping along the road pulled me back to the very real danger. Weston was heavily concentrated on driving. Solomon was locked up because of me and in that time Soren had attacked me and when he returned, I killed him.

Shot him.

Point blank.

In the face.

I closed my eyes.

My head pounding and my body hurting as the car began to jumble on the gravel roadway.

Somehow I managed to fall asleep or die, which would have been a blessing.

Then again, God didn't owe me any favors.

I was sitting on the rock face with Jake again.

The beautiful autumn now decayed.

His face paler.

"What is it?" I asked.

"I tried."

"What?"

"To save you." I reached out and gently squeezed his shoulder.

"You did everything you could for me, but it's okay. I'm ready."

"But I'm not," he whispered.

"What do you mean?"

"I'm not ready to let you go."

"You threw me off a boat and now you don't want to let me go?" I teased. He looked at me seriously; he didn't find it funny at all.

"You don't understand." His eyes were haunted, there was something he knew that he wasn't saying, but I was more than ready to be done with Solomon and the fight to survive him.

"Once it's over, we will be together, with mom. I won't have to keep going back and forth." I took his hand in mine and squeezed it gently. Looking down at it a gasp escaped me as I realized he was fading away. His eyes met mine.

"I'm sorry," he said quietly.

"No. I don't understand."

"I have to go."

"Jake, what's going on?" A single tear slid down my face, and he reached out his hand. Now it was nothing more than a phantom and I felt it briefly touch my cheek and swipe the tear away; I could see through him. As his thumb passed over my cheek, the tear disappeared along with him.

"Jake?"

He was gone.

CHAPTER
36

When the car stopped, I opened my eyes. Weston came around from the driver's side and reached in, dragging me out of the car. I tried to fight him as he pulled me out, my strength returning with the little amount of sleep I had. Fight or flight as they say. He grabbed my wrists and bound them together with one of his large hands. Instantaneously my mind put me back in that moment in the backyard with Soren and I squeezed my eyes shut, willing the horrid memories away. I didn't want to go back to that day, although I knew that it would live within me for the rest of my life, no matter how short.

"Come on." Dragging me down the gravel path, I stumbled over rocks and roots hidden in the snow, as we entered the trees.

As I looked around I could see treetops above us as the moonlight glimpsed up above them, casting light on the gentle snowflakes falling from the sky. They entranced me. At least I had something to keep my mind focused on. Just on the other side of those treetops somewhere, deep beyond this physical world, my mom and Jake were waiting for me.

When we made it to an opening within the woods, he stopped and threw me down against a fallen log. I scrambled to my knees. Before I could get my feet underneath me he delivered a swift kick to my side, a sickening crack shot pain through my body. I landed face down in the snow, breathing heavily as my lungs forced pressure on my broken ribs.

Pain seething between my teeth

"Now we can finish what you started." I wrapped my arm tightly around myself as I used the other one to push myself up, groaning as I got to my knees again.

"You never know when to stay down." I looked at him and watched as he cocked his head to the side. I couldn't tell if it was intrigue or he meant to mock me.

I didn't care.

As long as there was air in my lungs, I was going out on my own terms, but I wouldn't do it sitting down.

He took Jake from me.

Jake would want me to fight until the end, no matter what the odds. Unsteadily I rose to my feet.

"You really think this ends on your terms?" He laughed. "You can't win. Why do you keep fighting?" I took a deep breath, closing my eyes as Jake's voice came into my mind.

"You never give up. Never back down." Opening my eyes I stared at Weston. I stood firm, I wasn't going to back down, despite my mind screaming for me to run. I knew that as long as he had me in his sights, there was no getting away.

He came at me quickly, I tried to move away from him but wasn't fast enough as he grabbed me by the front of my jacket, using the velocity to pick me up and throw me down on my back. My shoulders hit the log, snapping my head back against the dense wood. I groaned as I rolled off falling onto the ground, letting myself lay on my side in the snow. The snow offered little relief from the pain in my body. He wasted no time as he began to deliver several blows with his boot to my stomach and chest. I tried to curl myself into a ball, but it didn't help, the internal damage had already been done. I coughed and on the ground, blood spewed from my parted lips, staining the snow a crimson red, that even in the dark was evident. He backed up and I looked up at him as he slicked his hair back as it had fallen out of place. I lifted my head and moved my arms from around myself so that I could grip at the ground to get myself back up.

Once back on my feet I stood, triumphant, this was going to end now.

"Why do you keep standing?" I stared at him, cocking my head slightly as I smugly shrugged my shoulders at him. We both knew how this was going to end, two of us came in and only one of us was going out. We both knew who it was going to be, I wasn't in denial of my impending doom, but I would be damned if I made it easy on him. Solomon wanted me to suffer, but what he failed to learn about me after all this time is my determination is strong. Taking Jake away from me was the fuel that fired my will to keep going and make my brother proud, until the bitter end.

I could feel the unmistakable drip of blood that was slipping from the corner of my mouth. My time was near, and I could feel it as my body began to sway. There was a pulsation deep within me that was unfamiliar, mostly a sign of catastrophic damage. I started towards him when he effortlessly reached out. He turned me, slamming me back against a tree. My head bounced against it. Dark spots began to dance behind my eyes as the moonlight seeped in through the hallowed treetops. His arm heavily against my sternum as he pushed me up, the toes of my shoes just barely scraping the roots of the tree where they began to leech into the ground.

"It's cold out here." A rattling in my chest forced me to cough, this time spewing blood droplets into his face. He ran the back of his arm across his mouth, wiping away the sprayed blood, irritation flashing like a warning sign in his eyes.

"There's only one problem," he sneered. I cleared my throat.

"What?" I cocked an eyebrow at him, wondering what other possible issues there could be. Everything was ending soon as he held me here, in the cold snow, the night growing more frigid with every minute.

"You are still breathing," he replied with a laugh.

There was a rustle from nearby and he turned his head, looking back the way we had come. The moonlight lit up the sadistic smile that appeared on his face as he looked back at me. I peered around him and saw a hooded figure lingering in the dark.

"Right on time."

The hooded figure walked towards us. Each footfall cracked the snow.

Deliberate.

Inevitable.

Weston released me.

I nearly collapsed, my legs shaking, but caught myself on the tree behind me. He turned away.

This was it.

My only chance.

I forced my body into motion, ignoring the agony ripping through every nerve.

Every stride was fire.

The tree line glimmered just ahead.

Freedom close enough to taste.

A hand clamped down on my arm.

I twisted, panic in my throat, and found myself staring into the hooded man's shadowed face. He yanked me back, hard. My feet scrambled on the ice, the rough bark biting into my palm as I caught myself.

He shoved me hard, pinning my arm behind me. A broken whimper escaped me as Weston's lighter flared, sparks briefly flashing, a single blue eye with a scar.

Sam?

Something flickered in my chest.

A memory.

Fear.

Hope.

Weston clapped, his laughter cruel and gleeful. "Do it."

The hooded man tilted his head like a puppet pulled by strings.

"Don't hesitate," Weston sneered.

A twisted smile stretched across the hooded figure's face in the dim light as he drew something from his coat.

Moonlight caught steel.

"Sam, don't."

The blade plunged into me.

White-hot agony detonated through my chest.

My cry split the silence.

As my body shook, I looked down.

His hand remained, holding it there.

Forcing me to feel.

Every.

Single.

Second.

His hood slipped.

Hair short.

Beard gone.

Through tears, I searched his face. For a breath-less, shattering moment...

I saw him.

He blinked, his gaze flickering, caught between shadow and memory.

"You see now?" Weston laughed, savoring it.

The eyes before me were lighter than I remem-bered.

Then it hit me.

Cold.

Brutal realization.

My lungs locked.

Heart freezing.

"No.. it." I stopped.

The name tore from me.

Desperate.

Chilling.

"Jake."

CHAPTER
37

"What did you call me?" he growled.

"Jake. That is your name," Weston cackled.

Jake blinked hard, rubbing his fingers across his eyes. When his gaze returned to mine, they were the clear blue I remembered.

"Jake." My lips trembled as his name escaped again, tears of joy colliding with the pain staining my face. He stumbled back, tears beginning to glisten in the moonlight. Recognition flickered as he staggered, breath strangled.

"Isabel?" A single tear cut down his cheek. He looked at his gloves soaked in red. He ripped them from his hands, tossing them into the dark. His eyes fell to the handle jutting from my jacket.

His gaze snapped to Weston, wild.

"What the hell did you do to her?"

Weston laughed. "You did this."

Jake shook his head violently. "No. No, I didn't."

Weston pulled out his phone, smirk curling. "Watch."

The screen glowed pale against the night. Weston tilted it toward Jake and pressed play.

The video was grainy but merciless.

Jake's hand on the blade, driving into my chest.

My cry.

Weston's horrifying chuckle as he filmed.

Jake froze, eyes wide, lips parting soundlessly. His breath hitched, broke, then vanished altogether.

His knees buckled, and he sank into the snow.

"No..." His voice cracked, barely audible. "No, that's not. That's not me..."

But the proof was there, flickering in the cold glow.

The phone slipped back into Weston's pocket.

Jake didn't move, body shaking as he stared at the blood staining the ground.

Weston crouched, patting his shoulder mockingly. "You remember now?"

Jake didn't answer.

"You can't unsee it." Weston leaned closer to Jake than I had ever seen him dare. "This is who you are."

Jake refused to look up, the truth chaining him to the ground.

Weston rose slowly and turned to me, the handle protruding from my chest like an invitation.

His whisper was hot in my ear.

"This is where it ends. Slowly."

With one swift motion, he wrenched the blade free.

The pain was blinding.

My scream ripped into the night, raw and sharp.

Blood gushed hot beneath my fingers as I collapsed at the base of the tree. My vision blurred, the snow beneath me churning black and red.

"No!" Jake yelled.

Behind Weston, Jake stayed on his knees. Frozen. Shaking. Silent tears streaked down his face as Weston lifted the dripping blade into the moonlight.

"Look at it," Weston sneered. "Your hands did that."

I could feel myself slipping, my head lolling as I tried to keep my eyes on Jake. He still didn't move. It was like the video had locked his limbs in place, his mind caged between guilt and disbelief.

Weston's attention shifted. His grin crooked at a sound from the woods. A dry stick cracked somewhere beyond the tree line, sharp, sudden.

Jake's eyes flicked up at the noise. For the first time since the phone screen, there was a tremor of life in them, a spark breaking through the paralysis.

He surged off his knees, snow scattering beneath him, and swung. A right hook connected with Weston's jaw, the crunch sharp and wet. Weston's head whipped sideways, blood spraying from his mouth. The gun relinquished into the snow.

Jake didn't stop. He slammed into Weston, driving him back, both of them crashing into the drift. They rolled, fists flying, snarls ripping through the night. Crimson stained the snow.

I tried to focus, my breaths coming in short, gurgling gasps. My chest burned with every movement, blood soaking my jacket. Through the blur, I caught flashes of them, Weston's teeth bared,

Jake's face twisted with fury, blood streaming from both.

"You cannot save her," Weston growled, dragging him into a chokehold. He yanked Jake upright, pinning him so I could see his face. "You never could."

Jake's lip was split, blood smeared across his cheek, condensation billowing with each ragged breath. His eyes locked on mine, burning even as his body trembled under Weston's grip.

I pressed my hand harder against the wound, shallow gasps rattling from my chest, tears slipping warm down my frozen cheeks. His eyes met mine. There was nothing either of us could do.

He knew it too.

But then something flickered behind those piercing blue irises.

Fire.

Jake snapped his head back, smashing into Weston's nose with a sickening crack. Weston howled, stumbling, blood streaming. Jake twisted free, scrambling to his knees.

Weston reached down.

Snapped back up.

"That's enough!" he barked, shoving a magazine into the retrieved gun with a hard click. He raised it, leveling the barrel at Jake.

Jake rose slowly, hands up, chest heaving, blood dripping from his lip. His eyes darted past Weston to me. I forced myself upright against the tree, swaying but standing. I couldn't let Weston take him away from me.

Not again.

Weston laughed, wiping the blood from his mouth with the back of his arm, grinning darkly.

Jake's brow furrowed.

"What?"

"Watching you stab your sister was the highlight of my night." His laugh was sharp and cruel. "Solomon will enjoy the video."

"You sick son of a bitch, I'll—" Jake snarled.

"You'll what?" Weston snapped, waving the gun. He paused for a beat. "I have already won."

Jake's gaze flicked over Weston's shoulder, meeting mine. I nodded faintly, letting him know I was still here. His shoulders sank.

We both knew the truth.

We were out of time.

I was out of time.

Weston adjusted his grip on the gun, as though execution was routine. "Now we stop pretending, son."

The barrel tracked Jake's chest.

"No," I whispered, my voice ragged. My knees trembled beneath me, blood soaking into the snow. I pressed against the tree for balance, lungs rattling like they were filling with fire. Every breath came sharp, wet, broken.

Jake's hands stayed raised, his gaze flicking over Weston's shoulder to me. I saw the plea in his eyes.

Don't move.

Don't do it.

But I couldn't listen.

I wouldn't.

"There are still people who will fight to see you pay for this," Jake spat, voice cracking with fury.

"You are right," Weston sneered. "They are not here, and you are out of time." He racked a bullet, grin widening. "Say goodbye."

The world narrowed to the trigger.

To Jake's wide blue eyes.

To the promise of losing him all over again.

"No!" I screamed.

I pushed off the tree and staggered forward. My legs felt like splintered glass, but desperation carried me. The snow blurred under my steps, my chest burning, vision tunneling.

Jake's voice tore through the night.

"ISABEL! STOP!"

I didn't stop.

I couldn't.

I had lost him once.

I wouldn't let it happen again.

I was already dying.

He had a chance at life again.

He was here.

He was alive.

After all of this time.

After everything he did.

He deserved to live.

For a moment, everything slowed, Weston pivoting, gun swinging toward me, Jake's face twisted in terror, my own breath catching fire in my chest.

My scream ripped free as I lunged, every ounce of strength poured into one final charge.

A shot in the dark.

Gunfire.

The flash lit the woods.

The report shattered the silence.

CHAPTER
38

"Don't fucking touch my kids."

The voice cut through the trees like the gunshot. My body locked, chest jerking as each breath scraped up through my throat. Weston writhed in the snow between Jake and me, a dark shape squirming in pain, crimson staining the snow under his right leg.

From the shadows, Uncle Ben appeared, pistol raised, his steps sure, snow crunching under his boots. He strode up, kicking the pistol out of Weston's reach.

"Don't move," he barked.

Then another light.

Dad.

His flashlight swung across the trees.

A torch in the black, landing on us.

The moment the beam hit Jake, my father dropped it low, stumbling forward, his face breaking apart as if disbelief had turned him inside out.

"Dad," Jake choked.

And then they collided. My father's arms around him, his lips planting desperate kisses into Jake's hair, his body shaking with sobs.

"I knew it," Dad gasped. "I knew it in my heart."

I stood watching, legs trembling, chest sawing, and for one second I let myself feel it. My brother was alive. He was here. A smile tugged weakly at the corners of my blood-cracked lips.

Then the sirens cut through the night, distant, closing fast.

"You hear that, you fucking prick?" Uncle Ben snapped, eyes never leaving Weston. "They're coming for you. They'll make sure you never see the light of day again."

Weston groaned, his face curling up into that smile.

The one I hated.

His eyes slid toward me, pinning me where I stood.

The pain came roaring back, searing my chest as the adrenaline bled away.

I was still dying.

The smile slipped from me as the metallic tang coated my tongue, blood running slow and bitter from my nose into my mouth. My lungs dragged, heavier with each inhale bubbling against the fluid inside me. But I couldn't look away from them. Dad clutching Jake, shaking with relief. I wanted that moment for them. Just a moment more, before I tore it all apart by leaving.

"Bel, you okay?" Uncle Ben's voice quivered. Dad and Jake turned at once, the flashlight beam cutting across me like a blade. Dad's breath hitched at the sight. He reached out instinctively, beckoning me closer.

I tried to move. My knees buckled. I wrapped my arms tightly around myself, as a cough tore up from deep inside me and splattered the snow with red. Droplets steamed faintly against the cold.

"Isabel?" His voice broke, staring at the crimson bloom at my feet.

"Daddy... I don't feel good." The words rasped out, rough and alien.

His eyes widened. "Your voice. You got your voice back." His relief lasted only a blink before fear hollowed it out.

My legs crumpled.

My knees slammed into the snow.

I curled tighter around myself as the pain twisted back, sharp, and merciless.

"Isabel!" Jake's voice cracked, wild with panic. He moved past Dad, crashing through the snow towards me.

Weston's laugh slithered from the ground. "You are too late."

"Shut the fuck up," Uncle Ben snarled.

The flashlight slipped from Dad's hand, tumbling into the snow, casting a weak sideways glow. He was beside me in an instant, dropping to his knees. Jake pulled me into his arms, my head falling against his chest. Each breath I took rattled, gurgling as it fought through the blood inside me. His hands shook as they pressed against me, then pulled back slick, glistening.

"Fuck," Jake sobbed, kissing the top of my head, holding me as if he could anchor me there by force.

"I told you she would not make it." Weston laughed again until Uncle Ben's boot shut him up with a grunt.

Dad wrapped around both of us, arms encasing his children. His shoulders convulsed. His voice a growl. "You're lying."

"The damage is done," Weston wheezed through blood. "You did this boy. Remember that."

My eyes met Jake's.

Dad looked between the two of us, searching for answers.

"Jake?" His voice riddled with guilt from asking.

Jake's eyes drifted to Dad.

The sorrow in them.

His silent confession.

Blinking back to me he absent mindedly pushed my hair back.

This wasn't his fault.

It was mine.

From the beginning.

The sirens sharp as they swelled closer.

To me they sounded as though they were fading.

My vision blurred.

The moonlight fractured in my eyes as everything shimmered.

"Hang on, Isabel," Jake pleaded, his tears wetting my hair.

I forced my gaze to Dad. "I'm sorry, Daddy."

"No. No, baby, no. You're going to be okay," he begged, rocking me against him.

"Mike!" Uncle Ben shouted, urgency in his tone, needing orders.

"Get help!" Dad's voice ripped apart as he clutched me tighter.

"There is nothing left to save," Weston croaked, laughing through evident pain.

Jake's arms stiffened. He lowered me gently into Dad's lap, stood, and staggered toward Weston. He ripped the gun from the snow, his hands trembling so hard it rattled.

"You motherfucker!" His scream cracked like thunder.

"Jake, don't!" Dad's voice cut, ragged with terror.

"Go on," Weston goaded, a smile creasing on his lips. "You want to."

Jake's finger twitched on the trigger. His breath came fast, clouds of steam in the air.

"You used me," Jake growled.

"It worked." Weston's smirk split the blood across his teeth. "Now she dies."

Jake's jaw clenched. "If she dies, you die!"

"Jake," Dad's voice pleading. "Come back. Please."

"Even now you cannot pull the trigger," Weston rasped. "You never finish anything."

Jake's eyes darted back to me. My chest shuddered, blood spilling from my lips, streaming warm down my chin. His face broke, fury overtaking his grief. He turned back and snarled.

"Shut the fuck up!"

The gun crashed down, smashing into Weston's temple and rendering him unconscious.

Silence followed, except for Jake's ragged panting.

"Jake…" It came out wet as my lips parted weakly.

He dropped the weapon and rushed back to me, his hands trembling as they brushed the matted hair from my face. He swore, though it sounded like a prayer.

His arms wrapped around me, his chest heaving like it was about to split. His words tumbled out between strangled breaths.

"I'm sorry," he croaked. "God, I'm so sorry."

"I know you would never hurt me." I pressed my lips together, the blood heavy in my mouth, forcing the words out in a shaky breath. "Jake… it wasn't you. It was him." I stopped as breath and blood mingled together. "It was always him."

He shook his head violently, hot tears splattering my skin.

"No. I hurt you. I should've protected you, and instead…" His voice broke, collapsing into a shaky whisper that sounded younger than I'd ever heard him. "I did this to you."

His sob hitched, rough and desperate, as though he was trying to swallow his own grief before it swallowed him. "I don't deserve your forgiveness."

My fading voice trembled like brittle glass. "Jake, you're my brother." I quivered, swallowing, to clear my throat. "You already have it."

A shallow breath rattled through me.

My body jerked.

Convulsions seizing me.

"Stay with me," Jake begged.

Snowflakes melted against my skin, but I couldn't feel them anymore. Jake's tears splashed hot onto my face, sliding down into the blood on my lips.

My lungs heaved one last time.

Choking.

Drowning.

Fear spiked through me, then bled out, replaced by stillness.

"Ben, hurry!" Dad roared into the trees.

Jake kissed my head again and again, frantic.

Then it came.

A light.

Not from the flashlight.

Brighter.

Softer.

"Please," Jake whispered.

A heartbeat thundered.

I opened my eyes, peeling my face from the frosted glass, gentle snowflakes dancing as we glided down the road. I turned to Jake as he kept looking over at me.

"What?"

"Seatbelt. Please." I reached behind me without breaking eye contact, pulling the strap across my body and clicking it. There was something distant in Jake's eyes.

"You okay?" He looked at me and gave me a sideways smirk, then reached out and ruffled my hair. I batted at him; he laughed as I swiped away the loose strands putting them back in place.

"Cut it out." I nudged him with my elbow.

"You pick it, kid," he said. "Grass or gravel?"

I laughed, free and breathless. He smiled as he began to laugh. For one heartbeat, I believed it was real. That nothing had ever gone wrong. That we would get the lives we were supposed to have.

But the road melted away as the light took over.

A flash.

A shock ran through my body.

The shadows departed.

With one faint, final thump in my chest, the laughter died into silence.

Thump.

Thump.

"I've got a pulse!"

ACKNOWLEDGEMENTS

To the Amazing Team at Golden Light Publishing House, Yvonne Hamilton and B. Wills, thank you for putting up with my crazy. Our crazies match and I love it! Love you ladies!

Racheal Shantel, my ride or die through this journey. I love our events together and looking forward to continuing this sisterhood with you. Love you Big!

The Chaos Crew, never could I have imagined that I would meet a group of strangers that became family. I am forever grateful that we all found each other. Love you guys!

To Dwayne, my rock, my anchor, my support, my love. There are not enough words in the world for me to show you how grateful I am to have you by my side as I have followed my dreams. Your unwavering support and love guide me through the dark. I love you.

To my family and friends, thank you for your continued support. I am so lucky to have such loving people in my life, some from the beginning and some that have been picked up along the way. Each and every one of you means so much to me.

To my fans, you guys are the real MVPs, reading, reviewing, giving me the feedback I need to make the stories stronger and thrive for you to enjoy. Without you there wouldn't be a Hunted Series. Thank you.

ABOUT THE AUTHOR

S Lynn C

S Lynn C is 34 years old, and lives in Ohio. An avid animal lover, with the dream of writing since she was 13.

She is the Author of Hunted: The Isabel Twain Story and is debuting her first dark romance.

S Lynn C signed with Golden Light Publishing House in 2025.

ALSO BY

S Lynn C

Hunted: The Isabel Twain Story
Abducted – Book 1
Into the Storm - Book 2
Secrets in the Silence – Book 3

Musically Yours Series
Pound for Pound

More Coming Soon...